Murde

A Madison Leigh Murder Mystery ....

Book One of the Madison Leigh Murder Mysteries

M J Parsons

Sign up for V.I.P. Updates

including new books and special offers at

mikeparsons.uk

Contents

Murder at the Marina

Chapter 1

I shut the door behind me and heaved a sigh of relief.

Perhaps it wasn't relief. Maybe it was more a sigh of despair and resignation.

"That's it then!" I said out loud as I looked around my new world. I was in the box room at Lengthsman's Lodge, my childhood home. A stunning seven feet square. Long enough for a bed, wide enough for a dressing table. No hanging space, I would have to share Jasmine's wardrobe.

I'd had an accident a couple of months ago. I was out of hospital, but I couldn't face returning to university, not yet. I was back in the house of my childhood, a place I never thought I would live in again. Mum died back in February, while I was still laid up in hospital. I'd missed her funeral. My sister, Mary, organised it, a fact that she will not let me forget for a long time. Joe, Mary's sixteen-year-old son, had taken over my old room. I couldn't turf him out, that wouldn't be fair. Jasmine, who was nearly five, offered to share her room with me, bless her. I couldn't burden her with a whinging aunty. I couldn't stay in the annexe, where mum used to live, as in their wisdom Mary and her husband Pete were in the process of re-decorating it, so they could let it out as a bed and breakfast. As a result, it was currently uninhabitable.

So there I was, Madison Leigh, fed up, hurting, and grumpy.

I leaned my walking stick against the dresser. I was determined to do away with the crutches I had been using in the hospital. Although I would never admit to it, there were moments when I would have welcomed them. I heaved my suitcase up onto the bed.

There was no-where else to put it. I winced as a sharp pain shot up my leg. I sat on the bed, joining my case, and rubbing my tender thigh. One consolation—this room was at the back of the house and looked down the garden to the canal at the bottom and beyond. It's a lovely view. When I was young, especially when it was raining and I couldn't go out, I would come in here and spend hours looking out of the window. It's a view I've never grown tired of. There's a mooring at the end of the garden, but no narrowboat. Mum and Dad used to have one when Mary and I were young. Those were the only family events I looked forward to—holidays on the canal. But we didn't go out nearly enough. Once I hit my teens, I took the boat out on my own. I wasn't happy at home, and it was like a taste of heaven. I was even allowed to stay out overnight as long as I didn't go beyond the locks. Mary never came. She wasn't into narrowboats the way I was. Then dad sold it. I cried when it was taken away.

Next door had a boat. They'd gone off cruising the canal network and put their cottage up to let. Some sort of mid-life crisis, I guess. I'd have lived there, but it was way out of my price range, even with mates-rates. In fact, everything was out of my price range. I had no money, and no job, and a leg which hurt like hell, so I was unlikely to get a job even if I wanted one. As you see, you're not meeting me at my best.

There was a timid knock at the door.

"Aunty M?"

It was Jasmine.

"Hey," I said, "come in."

She came in, looked around and pulled a disapproving face.

Jumbo, her terrier and devoted protector followed. He also checked out the room to make sure his small mistress would be safe. Once satisfied, and without invitation, he jumped up on the bed and settled down.

"It's a bit small for you," Jasmine said. "Are you sure you don't want to share with me—it'll be fun, and I don't snore like Daddy."

I couldn't help smiling. She was a treasure.

"Thank you, but I'll be fine here. It'll be lovely and cosy," I lied, "once I've got it sorted out." I rubbed my leg. It was aching something chronic again, but it was still another hour before I could take my meds.

Jasmine came and sat next to me.

"I'm sorry you're not well," she said.

"I'm okay. It hurts a bit, and that makes me a bit grouchy. I'll try not to be when I'm with you."

"That's okay. You can if you want."

She was such a sweet. It amazed me that Mary and Pete, two of the most selfish, self-absorbed people I knew, were able to produce Joe and Jasmine, two of the most wonderful people I knew.

"And the view from here is great," I said, nodding to the window and trying to look on the bright side. "Is Joe back from school yet?"

"No, he goes off with friends. Gets back in time for tea, usually."

Ah—I knew how he felt. That's what I used to do. I never saw eye to eye with mum and dad, so I went off with friends, or for walks, or hung around the local marina, which was not far away, anything to avoid home. Mary, on the other hand, was the goody-two-shoes who never did anything wrong. I think I was a mistake, and my parents never forgave themselves—or me.

"Do you want to come out? Me and Joe have cleaned up the pillbox and got some furniture. It's our den."

"It sounds lovely, sweetheart, but I can't walk any more for the moment. I need to rest my leg. Later maybe."

The pillbox was a small concrete bunker built during the war. It was pretty miserable inside, but from what I'd heard, the kids had done a grand job sprucing it up.

"Did they send the man who hurt you to jail?"

"No," I laughed. "It was an accident. I stumbled into the road and got hit by a bus. It was my own fault." My second lie to her in less than ten minutes. It was true that I was hit by a bus, but I was pushed by my ex-boyfriend, Liam, after an argument. I wondered what gossip Jasmine had heard to ask that question.

I hugged her and said I'd be down later. She went off, closely followed by Jumbo, and I lay on the bed, as best as I could with the suitcase, wallowing in self-pity.

My phone buzzed. A text.

I took a look without moving from my awkward position.

Damn it was Liam again. He was a right pain. It would be nice to think that he was contacting me out of guilt and concern, but I don't think he knew what either of those were. He said he felt terrible about what happened, but with him, it was just words. His text said that the hospital had told him I'd gone home. He said he'd be down tomorrow to make sure I was okay. I was tempted to block his number, but if I did, he'd end up phoning Mary, or even worse, he would turn up unannounced. At least this way I knew what he was up to. I replied, telling him not to come and to leave me alone. I can't leave you alone, he replied, I love you and miss you.

Yeah, right.

I texted back and suggested he came down next week after I'd had time to settle in. He agreed. With any luck, by then he would have found someone else to annoy and would have forgotten all about me.

I sighed and stared up at the ceiling.

Maybe I should've stayed in hospital. I'd insisted on being discharged as I was going nutty, but now I was here, I was liable to go nutty anyway.

Chapter 2

The following morning I woke early. I sat at the dressing table, fixing my face. The bruising was almost invisible now. It had been extensive, looked terrible, and was taking ages to go. I brushed my hair. I've always been pleased with how well the auburn shades go with my olive skin, and my large dark eyes. I guess I'm not too shabby, in spite of what Liam used to tell me. The thought of him made me shudder.

I used to have to keep my hair a little past my shoulders—that was how he liked it. It was getting a bit too long now. It hadn't been cut for months. Getting my hair done might cheer me up. Maybe I'd go short this time—some kind of pixie? I sat and experimented, pulling my hair around to try out different lengths and styles, as I sat awkwardly looking in the dresser mirror. I decided that short all over wouldn't work. I fancied it short on one side—oooo! Shaved maybe? Hmmm, it might look good, but I wasn't brave enough.

I checked out my face regalia, two little ear hoops on the upper part of my right ear and a small nose stud. They'd had to come out while I was in hospital, but I'd put them back in yesterday, knowing I was coming home. I'd been worried that the holes would close up, but it was all good. I've got no tatts, thank goodness. I'm totally off tattoos, at least for the moment. Liam wanted me to have one of his name, and I so nearly did. I can't describe how relieved I am that I didn't, so take my advice: don't do it!

I went downstairs and made breakfast, a bowl of cereal. I couldn't be bothered to do anything else. I flipped on the TV and channel surfed as I munched. Pete was at work, Joe was at school. Mary had taken Jasmine to school and would be heading on to work from there. I had no idea how I would fill the day. All I'd got planned was to book in at the hairdressers, but I should have got up earlier to beg a lift. I felt lost and useless.

Jumbo jumped up on the chair next to me. I stroked him, and he looked at me with concerned empathy. How can a dog even do that? I laughed, and he wagged his tail as if to say 'that's better, you should smile more'.

"Hi, Madison." Mary came in.

"Oh, hi, I wasn't expecting to see you. Forgotten something?"

"No, I came back to see if you were up. I need to talk to you."

Uh-oh, this sounded ominous.

"Tea?" she asked.

"Go on then, the kettle's already boiled, I hadn't got around to making it."

She made two mugs, handed me one and sat at the table opposite me. This looked like a proper heart to heart, so I turned off the TV. You wouldn't recognise us as sisters. She was thirty-one, seven years older than me. She was pale with mousy hair and always seemed to look worried, annoyed, or both. Today she looked worried.

"Madison, I've been sorting out mum's stuff since she died, probate and the like."

"Yeah, thanks for that. I'm here now, so if you need any help?"

"Most of it's done." She shifted uncomfortably. "The thing is, we may have a problem with the house."

"The house?" I froze with a spoonful of cereal halfway to my mouth. "It's mortgage-free. It must be worth over four-hundred thousand?"

"It is. As part of probate, we had it valued at four-hundred and forty."

"Wow! That's good, Mary, don't look so worried." I gave her a grin. She didn't respond. I felt nervous now.

She grimaced and said, "You know under the terms of the will, her estate is divided equally between us? She used all her savings paying for the care home, and there's no inheritance tax. There's only the value of the house left, so you're due around two-hundred and twenty."

I wondered where this was going. We had talked about this before, but only in rough terms, as we didn't have a valuation for the house then.

"We would love to keep this house. We were brought up here, and it's such a beautiful area."

"Yes, I know. That was always the plan. It would be great to keep it in the family."

"You know Pete, and I are both self-employed. He's on a temporary contract, and my contracts are short-term. We simply can't get a mortgage large enough for us to be able to buy out your half, and we have no savings to add in."

Damn! When we talked about this before, they were confident they would be able to get a mortgage when the time came.

"Recently," she continued, "mortgage companies have tightened up."

I gave an uncomfortable laugh, "I was going to use my half to buy a place of my own. While I'm not working and I have no job history I'll never get a mortgage."

"I know, Madison. The only option is for us to sell up and split the cash."

I leaned back in my chair and fiddled with my ear hoops.

"It's okay. We can do that, Madison, it's no problem."

It was not okay. It was frigging well nowhere near okay. I knew what was coming next.

She carried on talking, "We wouldn't be able to afford anything around here, or in Tinderford, or Milton Heath—at least nothing big enough for the four of us. We'd have to move nearer Birmingham."

"But the kids would have to change schools," I frowned. "Jasmine's settled in so well in year one at the infants' school, and Joe is halfway through his A-levels!"

"Yes, I know—but we did come up with a solution."

"Go on," I sighed.

"We could raise a small mortgage so we could pay you seventy grand cash. Once the work on the annexe is complete, we'd let it out as a holiday let as we planned. We reckon it will do well. We could pay you one-third of the profits—so you'd have a small income too."

"One-third?" This was getting annoying—it seemed like I was

making all the compromises. "But I own half the house, so surely I own half the annexe?"

"Yes, but we've done all the work to get it up to standard, and we'll be doing all the letting, cleaning, advertising, that sort of stuff. We'd have expenses, and we'd have paid you the seventy grand upfront. It'd still be a pretty good amount. We reckon your share could average out at about five-hundred a month, maybe more," she gave a thin, unconvincing smile. "This is a popular area for business and holidays, and there's a shortage of places to stay."

I didn't say anything, I sipped my tea.

"You could use the annexe for free out of season, from October to March, whenever we don't have bookings."

"Cheers, sis." I shook my head. "I don't get it, though. You can only raise a mortgage of seventy, against a house worth nearly four-fifty?"

"No, it doesn't work like that. We can only take out a mortgage against our half, our two-twenty grand. We'd go for a mortgage of a hundred—we've got a few debts and stuff to sort out. The solicitor would transfer the house into our joint names, me and Pete, and you. If my half is in Pete's name too, we'll have a better chance at a bigger mortgage at a later date. You'd still be a joint owner. You'd have a registered interest, a fixed percentage of the proportion that you own. That way, when you do cash out, you'd get the benefit of any increase in house prices."

"Okay. I need to be clear, you're saying that either I agree to take seventy, or I make Joe and Jasmine homeless?"

"Not quite homeless, but that's about the size of it."

"When would I get the rest?"

"When Jasmine's eighteen? We can have an agreement drawn up."

"Eighteen? That's almost thirteen years!"

I sighed and wondered if Jasmine would survive living here that long.

"Unless we can increase the mortgage in the meantime. Our advisor says to try again in a couple of years."

There was silence.

"I'm sorry Madison, I know this must be a blow to your plans but we're not sure what else we can do."

More silence.

"If there is anything I can do to help, you only need to ask."

I sighed.

"There is," I said slowly. "Give me a lift to hairdressers!"

Chapter 3

I stopped halfway over the bridge across the canal. My freaking leg was giving me jip. What a shitty first day back this was turning out to be. I'd given up on the hairdressers. The less time I spent with Mary, the better, with the mood I was in. I stared down at the canal but didn't take in what I was looking at. The beauty and tranquillity were lost on me today. I'd told Mary I would need to think about it, but she knew what my answer would be as clearly as I did. How could I force Joe and Jasmine away from here? The only other option would be to insist on living in the annexe rent-free until they could re-mortgage. What fun that would be—not.

I hobbled on, leaning on my stick a little more heavily to try to ease the pain. I was beginning to regret coming out this far. Moving around a hospital was one thing; going out and about in the big wide world, a whole other.

Eventually, by taking it slowly and stopping a lot, I made it to Tinderford Marina and gratefully settled on a bench. This was one of my favourite places, overlooking the basin full of narrowboats. It was serene and calming, with enough going on to distract me from my thoughts. Often, in hospital, I would close my eyes and think of this view.

It wasn't long before a familiar and welcome figure approached.

"Hi, Maddy—how's tricks?"

Ah, that was the other reason I came all the way over here.

"Hi, Charlie."

We hugged. Merely seeing him again raised my spirits. It felt as if we had only been apart for a few days, not several months. Charlie was a semi-retired jack-of-all-trades who worked at the marina. Always cheerful, always a good word to say about everyone. Over the years he'd been the one person I could talk to, never judgemental, never critical. Considering he was in his sixties, he had a surprisingly good handle on the problems I'd had growing up. He often said that the stuff people had to deal with was the same now as it was fifty years ago. People problems were exactly the same; it was only the world that had changed.

"You're looking a bit glum, gel," he said as he sat next to me, "Your leg playing you up, is it?"

"It is, but that's not it."

I told him about my dilemma.

"That's horrible to come back to, after all you've been through," he said.

"The one poxy light on my whole crappy horizon was that money," I whinged. "I was hoping to get something I could call my own—no rent or mortgage to worry about. I could live on a shoe-string if I needed to, and get some crummy job in a coffee shop while I got my head together."

"Your head?"

"Since the accident, I haven't been able to think straight. I've got my dissertation to finish from uni, but I can't face it, not yet. I can't seem to concentrate, and I certainly can't face the thought of applying for loads of jobs. It's all so overwhelming, Charlie."

"It'll take time. But you worked so hard at uni, and done well from what you were saying at Christmas."

[13]

"Yeah, and they've been great over the accident. I've got an extension—but I want to get it out the way now."

"I'm sorry, Madison. Things aren't looking good for you at the moment." He put an arm around my shoulder.

"Humph!" I mumbled. I leaned on him and felt better.

We sat in silence, looking over the glistening water, narrowboats lined up in the sunshine, a gentle breeze, and the occasional quack of argumentative ducks.

After a while, I sat up, and Charlie reached in his pocket and took out a tin. I smiled and without a word took it from him. I opened it. Inside were his tobacco and cigarette papers. When I was young, he taught me how to roll a cigarette, and I'd got it down to a fine art. I've never smoked, but I discovered that rolling a cigarette was curiously therapeutic, and a useful skill at university. We'd be hanging around with the boys, and a one would invariably take out his baccy and rolling kit. I would grab the baccy off him, and before he'd even sorted out his machine, I'd have one rolled and ready. Admiration all around, and they'd think they were onto a winner with me, but the truth was, I would never go out with a smoker. Once I got together with Liam, he made me stop my little party trick.

I handed Charlie a perfectly rolled cigarette. He had a faraway glint in his eye as if he had a story in mind.

"When I was a young lad, not long on the ships," Charlie was in the merchant navy for decades, "we was unloading sugar in a port in West Africa. On the dockside was a line of cranes." He paused as he lit up. "They were all made in England, they were. All worked perfectly, but there was never any electricity to use them," he chuckled, "so we unloaded with the ship's derricks. The local stevedores in the port operated them. We let them get on with it and sorted out any problems that cropped up on the ship. The sugar was in these big hessian sacks, see." He held out his hands to indicated their size. "Big and very heavy they was. The derricks picked up about thirty sacks at a time, in a gurt net sling. One day I was out on deck having a fag and watching what was going on. A sling full of sacks was being swung over the side to be lowered down to the dockside. This particular swing was a bit more violent than most, and the sacks weren't stacked well. One fell out and landed on one of the poor buggers working forty foot below."

"Oh, Charlie!" I exclaimed.

"Well, my heart was in my mouth. The others working down below crowded around him and dragged the sack off the poor man. He hadn't been killed. He was badly injured, though, lying on the ground. Conscious, mind, but unable to move. Maybe his back was broke, I dunno. I watched for the ambulance to turn up, but it never did. There was a lot of shouting and waving. After a while, they dragged the man from where he was to about ten feet away, so the unloading on that derrick could continue, and they left him there."

"What?" I was incensed.

"Everybody ignored him. I think he was calling out or moaning, but there were so much noise and activity going on, and he was too far away for me to hear—and I had to get back to work, anyway. When I checked later that evening, he was still there, all on his own. Work had ended for the day, and all the others on the dockside had left."

"Oh, Charlie! What happened to him?"

"Don't know. The next day, I went to look, and he was gone. Maybe his family came for him. Maybe the dock authorities took him out and dumped him in the street."

We sat in silence for a bit as I thought about what Charlie had said.

"I'm a whinging, selfish bitch, aren't I?" I said.

"No, I wouldn't put it like that."

"I could've been paralysed by the bus, had a life-changing injury—at least my leg's getting better."

"That's right enough," he agreed. Charlie had a way of helping get things in perspective.

"I'm wallowing in self-pity, but I've been offered seventy grand in cash."

"And you never know when something may come along, unexpected like," he added, "and change your life."

Then something unexpected did happen—my phone rang. I didn't know it at the time, but that call was about to change my life.

Chapter 4

I had to stop and rest.

Apart from the aching in my leg, I was over-heating. I took off my jacket. We were having a welcome mid-April mini heatwave, which was difficult to dress for as the mornings were still chilly. The taxi had dropped me as far down the track as he could go. The driver was concerned and had offered to help me the rest of the way with my bags, but I wouldn't let him. I paid him off, and he turned around in an area reserved for guest parking, and I struggled on alone. In front of me was a gate with a sign: Ducks in a Row. Private Property. Access to Private Moorings Only. On my left was a building which looked like it was once a farmhouse, but now had a sign outside: Barrow View B&B.

I wrangled my case and bags through the gate. There were only fifty yards to go. I was tempted to do it in two trips, but I'd had enough of walking and wanted it done in one. I slung on my backpack, picked up my bags and walking stick in one hand, and took the handle of my case in the other. I gritted my teeth against the growing ache in my leg.

Having said all that, I was in a good mood. I had something to look forward to.

The phone call I'd received when I was with Charlie was from Isla. We'd been inseparable at school and had kept in touch over the years. She was one of my first hospital visitors after the accident. I'd dropped her a text to tell her that I was out of hospital and she'd replied saying what good news that was. Then she'd rung because she was looking for a favour. Isla lived on a narrowboat with her cat, Ember. She and her boyfriend, who lived in London, were off to Australia to visit her sister who'd emigrated last year. When she went away, neighbours usually looked after Ember. However, this time she would be away for a whole month, and she knew I was at a loose end, so she wondered if I would like to look after both her cat and her boat. She said if I wanted I could take her boat out cruising. She knew how much I loved boats, and I reckon she'd guessed how trapped I'd be feeling. A month on the water was an offer I couldn't refuse.

I hauled my stuff the rest of the way. Looking around at the tranquil, remote setting, it was going to give me exactly the peace I needed, and the time to think. This was going to be a blast.

Ducks in a Row consisted of seven boats moored in-line along the canalside. The public towpath was on the opposite bank. There was an electric hook up for each boat and a couple of taps for re-filling water tanks.

Isla's boat was the last but one on the right, nose to nose with the boat on the end. My new home was fifty feet long and six feet ten inches wide. I was enchanted. She was so pretty, red, with green coachlines picked out along the side, and decorated with flowers. She had a traditional stern, which meant there was not much room at the back, but a good-sized bow, perfect to sit out on in the evening and drink wine.

I smiled. All in all, I was delighted with my new home.

I dumped my suitcase by Isla's boat and went next door to find Freda on the Bradford Bell, moored up to her left. Isla had told me she would leave the key with her. I leaned over and knocked on the bow doors.

"Anyone home?" I called.

"Oh, hello," came a Scottish voice from inside. The boat rocked a little. The doors opened, and a cheerful, middle-aged, grey-haired lady emerged. "Hello, hello, I'm Freda," she grinned. "I've been expecting you. Isla texted me earlier to tell me you'd be arriving this afternoon." Her accent and demeanour were infectious. I liked her immediately. She got out of her boat, kissed me warmly on both cheeks and shook my hand vigorously. "I've been looking forward to having a new neighbour—not that I don't love Isla of course, she's such a sweetheart, but ye ken what I mean." I smiled to myself, wondering if I would need a Scottish-English dictionary before the day was out. I had no chance to respond, she was off again. "Oh, will you look at your case? Isla told me about your trouble, you poor wee lass. Let me help you into your boat with it. I wish I'd known when you were being dropped off, what with your poorly leg. I'd have met you at the taxi and helped."

"That's kind," I managed to squeeze in.

"It's nay trouble lass, nay trouble at all."

We walked along to the bow of Isla's boat. I tried to sneak a look through the front windows of the last boat in the row, but all the curtains were closed so I couldn't see if anyone was home. In no time, Freda had unlocked the door to my new home, my case and bags were on board and stowed in the saloon.

"Now, I must ask," she said, "are you a wee bit hungry? Just in case, I've made a little extra."

"I am hungry, but I'm vegetarian."

Her face lit up. "Oh lovely, so am I, so am I," she gushed. "D'ye like a wee bit of pasta?"

[19]

"Sounds amazing," I laughed, as I'd half expected some Scottish delicacy.

"Well settle yourself in lass, and come over when you're ready. D'ye drink wine?"

"Whenever I can," I assured her, grinning.

"Oh, I've a feeling we'll get along famously," she said as she left.

The boat seemed strangely quiet once she had gone. I had a look around. I'd not visited Isla since she had bought her boat, probably three years ago, so it was all new to me. It was fitted out in light oak, and with the boho style curtains and decorations that Isla had added, it had a warm cosy feel. The saloon was large. It looked as if there had originally been a dinette—seats and a table that could turn into a bed—but at some stage, Isla, or a previous owner, had removed it to expand the sitting area. The result was effective. There was a lovely sofa that converted into a good-sized pull out double bed, a multi-fuel stove in the corner by the bow doors, and a TV low down on one wall. The galley was functional but was looking a little tired and was probably due for a re-fit. There was a good-sized gas hob and oven, a fridge with a freezer section, and a microwave. On the worktop, there was a note from Isla, with instructions. I'd take a look at that later.

Down the narrow corridor was a sort of utility area with a couple of cupboards and some storage. There was a short curtain down low. I pulled it aside. Oh—a washing machine! I hadn't expected that, but it made sense. Isla spent a lot of the time moored up, with a cable connected to mains power. She didn't have to worry about her energy usage, so the washing machine was perfect.

As I straightened up again, I realised that this section of the boat had recently been re-fitted. The storage area and washing machine cubby hole looked purpose-built. Next was the bathroom which, of course, didn't have a bath. The shower was fantastic and more substantial than I expected. There was a gorgeous counter-top basin, a sturdy looking loo, and a heated towel rail. Finally, the bedroom. The bed was covered in a lovely flowery quilt that looked delightfully snuggly.

"Hello you," I said, as I spotted Ember lounging on the bed watching me. "I'm here to look after you for a few weeks. I hope you don't mind." Ember stretched and purred as I stroked her. She didn't seem to mind at all.

There was plenty of storage underneath the bed and hanging space in a small wardrobe. Although it contained Isla's things, there was still room for me. There was another TV on the bedroom bulkhead—what luxury!

I joined Ember on the bed, and it was as comfortable as it looked. This was going to be exactly what I needed, a break away from everything on a peaceful canal boat.

I was so happy, I could have cried.

"This is lovely, Freda," I said as I tried not to wolf down the pasta. I hadn't realised how hungry I was. It must have been all the travelling and fresh air. "There are seven boats along the moorings here, who lives on them?"

"Aye, well, let me see now. Beyond your boat, at the end, that's Harper on Red Rum." Her voice dropped a little as if she didn't approve of something. "He's not been here long and keeps himself to himself. The other side of me there's Jill and Adam, on the Wandering Cow, a lovely couple. You'll love Jill. Then it's Veronica and Alice on Madrigal. They have their niece, Rose, staying with them, and they have a lovely Scotty called Wiggles. He'll steer well clear of Ember—she had a go at him once, and he's never forgotten it! Then it's Carlton, on Bobby Dazzler. He's the chef up at Barrow View, a talented cook, so they say." She laughed and took another spoonful of pasta. "Don't be put off by his size. He's a braw big man, but kind enough. Then right up the other end is Danny and Paula's boat, 'Auf Wiedersehen'. They own the bed and breakfast and the moorings. They used to go out on her, cruising, but they've not done that for a long time. Occasionally they let people rent it, but I don't think they're supposed to."

"Sounds a lovely community," I said.

"It is, aye, that's what it is—a community. And tomorrow evening Jill and Adam are holding a barbecue for us all, so you can meet everyone."

"That's nice. I hope it's not because of me?"

"It is a bit for you," she grinned, "but we do have regular get-togethers anyway. I hope you're okay with that? You needn't come if you don't want to, but it's only over there on the canalside by their boat," she pointed.

"I will be pleased to come along. It will be lovely to meet my neighbours," I said, to her delight.

I headed home, full of pasta and wine, happy and perhaps a little tipsy, and looking forward to meeting the other neighbours. This was a surprise to me, as I'm not a great socialiser. Back on the boat, I locked the bow doors and went around the saloon and galley closing the curtains. I checked that Ember had food and water and cleaned up her litter tray. Then I crashed out on the sofa, read Isla's instructions, and watched some TV. Ember came and joined me, curling up on my lap.

"Well, you're not going to give me too much trouble, are you?" I said to her.

She purred and turned her head a little to encourage me to tickle under her ears.

That night, I snuggled into my bed, well-fed and happy. Ember was at the other end purring to herself, and for the first time that I could remember my leg wasn't aching. I smiled to myself. I was going to enjoy my time here. As I fell asleep, I silently thanked Isla for asking me to look after her adorable cat and her equally adorable boat, Mercury.

Chapter 5

You know what it's like when you sleep in a bed that you're not used to—restless, unable to settle, and you keep waking up? In hospital, I don't think I got one good night's sleep. The bed was uncomfortable, and it was noisy all night. In complete contrast, when I awoke on the boat the next morning, I'd had a lovely night's sleep—deep, dreamless and refreshing. I felt good—for the first time since whenever.

I lay in bed and looked around my narrow bedroom. I'd been on narrowboats plenty of times over the years. During the holidays I helped out at Tinderford Marina, showed hire customers the ropes, so to speak, and took them on test drives, but it was a long time since I'd slept on one. It felt comfortable and cosy, and the almost imperceptible rocking of the boat had gently lulled me to sleep.

Ember had already nosed through her catflap and gone off to explore. I stretched, sighed, and decided it was time for me to get up too.

During my visit to the bathroom, I couldn't resist trying out the shower. I was pleased to discover that Isla was as environmentally friendly as me, and there was a lovely range of eco toiletries to choose from. On narrowboats, shower trays are set a little below floor level, and well below the waterline of the canal. The problem is how to get rid of the wastewater, and the solution is a gulper; an unnecessarily noisy pump which takes the water up above the waterline and dumps it out into the canal. Water from showers and sinks is called 'grey waste', and it's allowed to go straight into the canal, but you can't go dumping anything in there.

We share the canal with our neighbours, the wildlife. You've no idea how annoyed I get when I find boaters not using eco washing-up liquid, soap, washing powders, that kind of thing.

The water was piping hot, and my shower proved to be as lovely as it had promised. I wrapped myself in a towel, with another around my hair. I opened all the curtains and made breakfast and a cup of tea. I was about to put the TV on when I kicked myself. Who in their right mind would sit and watch TV here? I took my breakfast onto the bow, so I could look out over the tranquil waterway and the countryside beyond. Only one boat passed—it was still early in the season, and it was school term time—but there were several ducks, four swans, and two herons further up on the opposite bank.

A knock on the side of the boat behind me startled me back to reality.

"Hello?" said a voice. "Sorry to bother you, I'm Rose." Standing on the bank was a young, somewhat nervous girl. "From along there." She pointed up past Freda's boat.

"Oh, yes, of course. Hi, I'm Madison. We managed an awkward handshake—I was still wrapped in towels after my shower. "Come on in, if you don't mind that I'm not dressed," I said as I headed back into the saloon.

"I can come back—" She made as if to leave.

"No, no need to go. Please don't. The kettle's hot. Tea? Coffee?"

"Tea, please." She came in and sat down. Almost immediately, Ember appeared from nowhere and jumped onto her lap. "I come around most mornings and drink tea with Isla. I hoped you wouldn't—" Her voice, already quiet, trailed off.

"Of course not. It's lovely to meet you. Milk?"

"A small drop, please." Ember was lounging all over her lap and purring louder than I'd ever heard before.

"She seems to like you."

"Aunt Alice has a dog, Wiggles. He's fun, but I prefer cats."

I sat down next to her. "Like any breakfast? Toast?"

"No, I've eaten thanks."

We fell into a slightly uncomfortable silence, disturbed only by the astonishingly loud sound of Ember's purring. Rose looked about fourteen. She was thin—too thin, pale, with mousy coloured hair. She wore red square-framed glasses, which she kept pushing up the bridge of her nose, even though they didn't need it.

"So you're staying with Veronica and Anne?"

"Um, Alice," she corrected.

We fell silent again, and I began to feel like a dentist, pulling teeth.

"Are you at school near here?" If she was, I wondered why she wasn't there. The Easter holidays ended over two weeks ago.

"My mum's in hospital. She's had an operation, but it didn't go that well, so I'm staying with Aunty Alice."

"I'm so sorry to hear that."

She carried on, embarrassed by my concern.

"I've got school-work to do. I send it in online."

"That's good. you'll be starting your GCSEs soon?"

"I'm taking them this year."

"Oh, sorry I—."

"That's alright. Lots of people think I look younger than I am. I took two early—last year. I've got the other six this year, in June. I'm revising."

"Did you do okay? Last year?"

"Yes, both grade nine, Latin and Chemistry."

"Nine? Is that good?" I've no idea what nine is.

"That's like an A-star. I expect I'll get nines for all the rest."

She spoke as if it were a dull inevitability, and didn't look pleased at the prospect. But I guessed that with her mother ill, that overshadowed everything.

"That's excellent. I got mostly Bs. How do you get on with your Aunt?"

"She's lovely. But I know I'm in the way. She and Veronica have their own life. I like the jewellery making though."

"Jewellery?"

"Aunty Alice makes jewellery, look!"

She unzipped her jacket and showed me a delicate silver pendant on a chain.

"She made that? That's fantastic."

Rose nodded and smiled a little.

"Where are you from?" she asked me.

"Oh, er, Tinderford."

"Not heard of it. What do you do?"

"I'm taking some time out, recovering from an accident."

"Oh dear, you had an accident?" She looked at me, her face full of concern. It was touching.

I explained to her what happened. As she sipped her tea, stroked Ember and listened, she defrosted a little. She asked questions, and we laughed at one point.

"You don't have a boyfriend, then?" she asked.

"Not at the moment."

"I like Harper, but I think Carlton's free."

"I'm not in the market, Rose. You like Harper? I got the impression he was older?"

"He is. He's in his thirties. I wouldn't want to go out with him—but he looks—erm, lush."

I couldn't help smiling. I unwrapped the towel on my head and shook out my hair.

"I need to run a comb through it before it dries."

"It's lovely Madison," she gasped.

"I was going to get it cut, but then I got the call from Isla and never got around to it."

"It could do with a bit of tidying up," she said. "I could cut it for you?"

I smiled and went to find a comb.

When I came back, she was beaming all over her face. She had put Ember on the floor, who was mincing off as if it was his idea all along.

"Sit," she said. She held out her hand for my comb, and with not a little concern, I handed it to her. She made me turn around and began combing it out.

"I do some of the girls' hair at school. It's the one thing I'm good at."

"Rose, it sounds to me like you're good at a lot of things."

"Not really. I can be a little shy."

"I hadn't noticed," I laughed.

She laughed too. She was like a different person. As soon as she began working on my hair, the anxious Rose disappeared. She was chatty and confident. She asked me what I had in mind. We discussed different styles, cuts, celebrity hair, and I soon realised that she knew exactly what she was talking about. Based on her knowledge alone, she could get a job with a top stylist tomorrow if she wanted. I tried to think of a polite way to ask her why her own hair was so boring and dull. She guessed my question and said she hated people touching her. She had no interest in making herself more attractive. She was scared of boys, and this way they tended to ignore her.

My text alert sounded.

"Hang on—" I said, as I grabbed my phone.

Damn, it was Liam. What the hell did he want? I read the text. He had heard that I wasn't at home and he was worried about where I was. He must have rung Mary. I decided to ignore him.

By now, I was convinced that Rose would do a good job. She told me she had been staying with Alice for two weeks, and this was the first time she had been able to talk to someone about hair. She would have made a start there and then, but I wanted to get dressed and do a few jobs, so we agreed she would come back after lunch to fix me up. When she left me, she was a different girl to the bag of nerves who had arrived. What a curious person she was. Still, she had achieved something in life that I hadn't. She had found something she loved doing, which sparked joy for her.

"Aye, she's an unusual wee lass," agreed Freda. "And ye're going to trust her to your hair?" she frowned.

"I am," I grinned.

"Rather you than me."

We were eating lunch on my boat. Isla had left it well stocked. I wouldn't need to go shopping for several days, and I wanted to repay Freda for her kindness. It was nothing special, a Greek salad with couscous.

"Tell you what," I threw down the gauntlet, "if you like what she does, let her do yours!"

"Are you saying my hair's a mess, you cheeky lass?" she laughed.

"You know what I mean. Go on!"

"I dinnae ken. She's barely said a word to me all the time she's been here."

"She's painfully shy. Give her a break."

"I'll have to love your hair, mind."

"Deal!"

I topped up our mugs. Freda said she didn't drink alcohol at lunchtime, which was a relief as I'd had a glass too much on her boat last night, so we tried out some fruit teas I'd found in the cupboard.

"She said she liked Harper?" asked Freda.

"Hmm. Said he was 'lush'."

Freda smiled and then turned serious. "She'd do well to steer clear of him."

"Not met him yet. What's he like?"

"What is it they say now? Candyfloss?"

"Eye candy," I laughed.

"That's it. He's a real heart breaker, Madison. He's wicked!"

"Is that wicked meaning good?"

"No lass. He's handsome and looks like butter wouldn't melt—but he's nasty."

She was serious.

"Why? What's he done?"

"Aye, well lass. I'm not one to spread gossip."

And she was right, as that was all she was prepared to say.

Chapter 6

Rose arrived soon after Freda had left.

We had a lovely afternoon. To my surprise, she brought her own scissors, combs and clips. After some discussion, we settled on a pixie cut. I must admit that I was feeling nervous. As I sat and waited for her to begin, I almost bottled out. Hair is so personal, and it suddenly dawned on me that if she messed up, I'd be distraught and feel worse about myself than I already did. I managed to hold it together and say nothing. I had agreed to this, and I would take whatever positives I could from it, but I must admit I closed my eyes and took some deep breaths during the first few minutes of scissor snips. Ember was highly bemused at all the strange activity, but after a while, she ambled over to the bed and curled up for a sleep.

During the afternoon, my text alert went off. It was Liam again. I would read it later.

In the event, to my huge relief, Rose did a marvellous job. She adapted the style to my hair colour and facial features with remarkable skill. All in all, I was delighted and more than a little impressed with the results and thrilled that I'd have smart hair for the barbecue.

"Rose, if you lived around my way I wouldn't let anyone else touch my hair," I said, as I examined myself in a mirror. "Seriously—I'm not just saying that."

I insisted on paying her, telling her it was no more than she deserved. She blushed and mumbled something as she took my money, reluctantly. I swept up my hair clippings while Rose packed up her kit, then she left.

The barbecue was due to kick off at around five. I decided on an afternoon nap. I don't usually like to nap in the afternoon, but with everything that had been going on, I was tired, and it was catching up on me.

I think it was the smell of smouldering charcoal that woke me. When I checked the time, I was surprised that it was gone half-past five. I freshened myself up and headed out, grabbing a couple of bottles of wine on the way.

"Hi, I'm Madison, a friend of Isla's," I said to the man at the barbecue as I handed my offerings to him.

"Thanks," he took the bottles from me. "I'm Adam, and this is Jill," he said, pointing out the woman who was approaching us both with a tray of bread rolls. "The barbie's almost up to heat. I'll start chucking things on. You're vegetarian, aren't you?"

"Yes. Impressed that you knew that."

"Freda told me—she is too."

"I saw you out the window yesterday," said Jill. "You've had your hair done since then, and it looks amazing. How did you manage that?"

"Rose did it."

"Rose? As in—" she pointed vaguely towards Madrigal.

I laughed at her reaction and confirmed that it was indeed Alice's Rose.

The evening was perfect. The weather stayed warm, the food was excellent, and the company was entertaining. I took to our hosts, Jill and Adam, at once. They were both in their mid-forties. He was a barman at a club in town. She was a graphic designer and worked from her boat. She was pretty, dark-haired, a little taller than me, but much funnier. She had plenty of hilarious risqué anecdotes. She and Charlie would be a scream together. You should always invite a Jill to a party.

Freda sat next to me, and after approving wholeheartedly of my new hairstyle, she announced that Rose was to do her next. Veronica and Alice soon joined us, bringing cans of beer and bottles of wine, with Rose trailing shyly in tow. I had a long chat with Alice about Rose, who couldn't believe what she had done with my hair. She said Rose had always liked to play hairdressers, but she had no idea that she was so talented. Rose smiled modestly and said nothing. Wiggles raced about and visited everyone in turn, begging for food. After a while, Rose took him off for a walk. Then Carlton appeared, and I had the opportunity to watch him as he chatted with Adam.

From Freda's description of Carlton being a chef and a braw man, I had been expecting something entirely different. He was certainly big—but not in the way I'd pictured. He was a black hunk, and it was all muscle. Judging by his body and its tone, there must be a gym somewhere nearby. He had a gorgeous chiselled face, a stubbled chin, and brown eyes to die for. He looked as if he might be a bit of a lad, but as soon as I got talking to him, it was clear that he was lovely. He was ex-army, a Rifles regiment. He told me that after he left the army, he re-trained as a chef, and he'd been working at Barrow View for almost a year.

[34]

He asked me if I'd been up to the long barrow yet.

"The long barrow?" I asked.

"A prehistoric burial mound. It's one of the largest in England. The bed and breakfast was named after it: Barrow View."

"Where is it?"

"The track starts next to the house. It's about a mile that way," he pointed. "Most of it was excavated years ago, but they still do digs round and about when they get the funding. I help out when I can. In the original excavation, over one hundred and fifty years ago, they found the remains of two bodies. They'd been undisturbed for several millennia."

"Millennia, eh?" I smiled to myself. I'd never have guessed he was a history nerd.

"From the items found with them," he carried on enthusiastically, "it was a man and a woman. When they were first uncovered, they were holding hands."

"That's lovely, but it's a shame they weren't left in peace."

"It is," he agreed. "But they had the last laugh. It's said that if you go down there at midnight, during a full moon, you can see their ghosts, kissing and cuddling in one of the side chambers."

I laughed and slapped him.

"Honest," he grinned.

Conversation flowed, covering all sorts of topics. Freda talked about her short marriage many years ago. This led to talk of other relationships, and the jobs various partners did, then jobs we'd enjoyed or wanted to do, and so on. Rose came back with Wiggles, and she listened intently to the conversation. The little dog bounded around, tail wagging, snuffling about for any dropped morsels.

Jill noticed me looking over at Harper's boat. There was a light on, but he hadn't come out.

"I doubt he'll join us," she said. "He keeps himself to himself."

"He's not been here long, has he?"

"No, a couple of months. There's a bit of a story. He—"

"Madison!"

While all this had been happening, dusk had crept upon the gathering. We were interrupted by a voice behind me that made my heart sink. I reluctantly turned to see Liam standing there.

With the lights from the boats and some lanterns, the canalside was a patchwork of shadows. I was glad no-one could see my reaction. For an instant, a split second, my heart leapt, and my instinct was to jump up and hug him and kiss him like I used to— then I remembered—I stared at him with my hand to my mouth.

Everyone fell silent and watched.

"Madison, I've been so worried about you," he gushed.

He leaned down to kiss my cheek, but I moved my head.

"What are you doing here?" I stuttered.

"I told you I was on the way. I sent a text."

Damn. The one I ignored earlier. I was in turmoil.

After a few moments, people started talking again. Adam offered Liam a drink. I pointed out that he was driving, but Liam said one wouldn't hurt. Adam tried to be a good host and took him off to the drinks table. Freda put a hand on my arm. I looked at her and rolled my eyes.

There was me, thinking things couldn't get any worse when Freda's hand tightened on my arm. I looked at her, and she nodded past my boat. A figure was heading towards us. I guessed it must be the infamous Harper.

Even in the shadowy darkness, it was apparent that he was a looker. It was also apparent that he knew it. Tall, dark and handsome didn't do him justice. Think Zac Efron, with a touch of Johnny Depp thrown in. He was around six foot tall, with a loose, confident gait. He was dressed shabbily, which had the effect of adding to his rough appeal. As he sauntered over, conversation stilled.

"Hi, Harper," Adam said. "Drink? Liam—Harper, Harper—Liam." he introduced them.

Liam put out his hand. Harper ignored him, and without a word, grabbed a bottle of beer from the table, opened it and took a swig. When he had walked past me, he had ignored me. Now he noticed me and made a beeline.

"Hi," he grabbed a chair and put it awkwardly in front of me, blocking me in. "Who's this?"

"Madison," Freda answered before I had a chance to.

"You've had your hair done since yesterday." He reached up and touched my hair. I pushed his arm away. He laughed.

In the corner of my eye, I saw Liam take a step forward.

"I'm turning in now," I said. I made to get up. Harper took my arm and hauled me to my feet. It was so unexpected, I was caught off balance. I tried to push him away, but before I could recover, he grabbed my chin with his other hand and held my face while he kissed me.

It all happened so quickly. His grip hurt. I struggled, but I couldn't stop him.

Then, I'm not sure what happened.

Two or three people shouted his name at the same time. Liam stepped up, and I think he put his hand on Harper's shoulder. Harper spun around to find Adam there too.

"Hey Harper—leave off will you?" Adam said.

I was trying to extricate myself, but I was trapped between Harper and the chairs.

He turned back to me.

"She's cute."

"Hey, man!" Carlton had joined the party and looked more menacing than all the others put together.

"Oh, the mighty Carlton has spoken," sneered Harper.

Had he been drinking? Maybe something else, as I couldn't smell alcohol on him.

"Leave her alone!" Carlton said.

"Or what?" Harper squared up.

Freda, who was also on her feet by now, moved her chair, so I could get out. We both escaped back to my boat and left them to it.

"Are ye alright, lass?" Freda asked once I was inside and sitting down.

"I'm fine—thank you." I was shaking a little more than I should have. I've been in the middle of fights before, and I wasn't sure why this one shook me up so much. Maybe because it came out of nowhere, or perhaps because I felt vulnerable with my leg, which was now aching like hell.

I calmed down quickly. I was cross with myself that I hadn't handled it better. I should have smacked Harper around the face, but likely he would only have laughed. If I hadn't got a bad leg, I'd have kneed him where it hurt.

We felt the boat rock, and I tensed up again, but it was only Liam.

He told us that Harper and Carlton had nearly come to blows. Carlton had started accusing Harper of something—nothing to do with me, and Harper had been laughing it off. Liam thought there must be something else going on between them. He told us that he and Adam had managed to defuse it. In the end, Harper had told Carlton to piss off and headed back to his boat. Carlton was left steaming and swearing revenge.

Freda left us, after assuring herself that I really was fine. All I had to do now was get rid of Liam. That was easier said than done.

"I'm so glad you're okay, Madison. I was worried."

"Liam, I've been worse. It's not a problem."

He sat next to me and took my hand.

[39]

"I've missed you. You know that, don't you?"

I shuddered and took my hand back. Ember wandered in. Cats seem to have an innate sense of who in a room hates them most, and then demands to be fussed by them, out of sheer spite.

"You may have—" I began, then at precisely that moment, without warning, Ember jumped onto Liam's lap, as if she had planned it.

"Ugh," he yelled and jumped up, dumping poor Ember unceremoniously on the floor.

"Hey, careful!" I yelled. I picked her up and calmed her down. She soon settled on my lap.

"I don't like cats," Liam grumbled, as he poured himself a glass of wine.

I sighed.

"I know, but that was a bit over the top."

He smiled and tried to look cool, which made me cringe. He was trying to get back into the mood—his mood, not mine. "I'm so glad you're okay. I came over here because—well—I've given this a lot of thought, and I think it's time we got back together again. I've missed you so much, and you know how upset I've been about your accident."

Was this his way of apologising, making it all about himself?

"Well, it wasn't so much of an accident, was it?" I said.

"When you tripped—"

"Well, I didn't trip, did I?"

"Yes, you—"

"You know you pushed me."

I tried to say it lightly—was he for real?

"You think I pushed you? Oh, no, poor Madison! No wonder you're upset at me. No, we were discussing what to do, and you tripped and stumbled into the road."

"Liam," I was getting cross, "you pushed me after you told me to f-off and not come back to your flat—which, by the way, was actually in my name—and I paid the rent!"

"Let's not worry about water under the bridge. I think it's time you came home."

"Oh, you think, do you? I think it's time you left!"

"I can't drive now. I've had a couple of drinks, and after that little episode out there I reckon it would be better if I stayed tonight."

"In your dreams! What part of 'leave me alone' don't you understand?"

"I know it's difficult for you, with your leg," he rested a hand on my head, "and I'm sure we can find some way to sort out this disaster—"

I shrugged off his hand.

"For goodness sake Liam, you're a freaking—"

I didn't get a chance to finish my sentence. He leaned in and kissed me—on the lips. I was raging and slapped him. Two unwanted kisses in one evening.

"Sleep in your freaking car!" I yelled.

In the end, I gave in and reluctantly said he could stay on the boat. He assumed I meant in my bed. I quickly put him right and made him set up the pull-out in the saloon. I found a sleeping bag, left him to it and went off to bed myself.

I couldn't sleep for ages. This was supposed to be a lovely relaxing time, a chance for me to recharge my batteries, and it was turning into a nightmare. It wasn't long before I felt the boat rocking. He must be moving around, going to the bathroom. I heard my bedroom door being tested, but I wasn't stupid. It was locked.

Eventually, I managed to drop off, but I couldn't get comfortable and kept waking up. At some point, I felt the boat rocking again. Maybe he couldn't sleep either. Tough.

I woke up the following morning, after an unsettled night. It was a little after eight. My head was thick and heavy. I think I had drunk more than I realised. I would have laid in bed for longer, but I needed the bathroom. I got up trying to make as little noise as I could. I didn't want to disturb Liam. I unlocked the door and edged down the narrow corridor. When I was done, I peeked around the doorway into the saloon. It was empty. To my huge relief Liam wasn't there. It was like a weight had been lifted from my shoulders. I instantly felt better and laughed out loud. Relief turned to delight when I found a note from him and realised that he had gone home. He'd written some stuff about last night. He had the audacity to tell me that he knew I still loved him, then he said that he understood that the accident had affected me, so he would give me more time to recover. I threw the note in the bin.

I grabbed my phone and debated, again, whether I should block his number. I decided not to. It would be easier to keep track of him. It hadn't worked yesterday, but that was my fault because I hadn't read the text saying he was coming down. I cleared up the bedding, pushed the pull-out bed away, and tidied the saloon.

I splashed water on my face, put the kettle on, opened the curtains and looked out at the day. Clouds were gathering ominously. It looked like the hot spell had broken and we might be heading for the first rain for over ten days. I made tea and looked forward to a peaceful day on the boat with Ember. Actually, after yesterday I could do with a peaceful week.

After breakfast, my head had more or less cleared, and I was feeling more social. I got dressed and decided to visit Freda, to get her take on last night's fiasco. I unlocked the bow doors to head out, but the doors wouldn't open. Something was in the way. I looked down, and for a split second, I thought someone had dumped a pile of clothes out on my well-deck. Suddenly I realised it was a person, and that person was Harper. He was curled up in a foetal position with his back against the doors. I thought he must be sleeping off a hangover.

"Harper!" I called through the small gap that I had created between the doors.

He didn't respond. I nudged him with the bow doors and called again, but still no response.

Something was wrong.

I went up to the other end of the boat, got out the stern door and walked around to the bow.

As soon as I stepped down into the well-deck, I saw it. I don't know how I hadn't seen it from inside.

Blood.

I leaned down and moved his arm. His button-up shirt was open, and I could see the source—protruding from his stomach was the handle of a knife.

He was dead.

Chapter 7

I don't think I can describe how distraught I was.

I'm not easily inclined to tears or outward shows of emotion, so I didn't cry. Perhaps that was more down to shock. I was no stranger to trauma. I'd travelled the world for three years before university, and seen many distressing things. However, it's a whole different level when a body literally turns up on your doorstep, and it's someone you know, sort of.

The morning passed in a haze. After discovering Harper, I told Freda. She stared at me, wide-eyed as if I had gone mad, and went to see while I phoned the police. I found a blanket and covered him. By this time, the commotion had brought Adam and Carlton out of their boats. Perhaps it was just as well that Veronica and Alice were out with Rose, and that Jill had left early on a client meeting.

The police arrived quickly, and over the following couple of hours they were joined by yet more police and others—cars, vans, and lots of people dressed in white, putting up tape and taking photographs—forensics, I presumed.

I retreated to Freda's boat. Later in the morning, a woman detective sergeant, Jackie Meade, came to speak to us both. She'd barely introduced herself when a forensics guy turned up and invited me back onto my boat to grab some essentials. They supervised me while I was aboard and logged the things I took—including the cat, who accepted the disturbance and disruption with her usual indifference. When I got back to Freda's boat, the DS explained that we would both need to make formal statements later, but at this stage, she wanted to piece together what had happened.

There wasn't much I could tell her. I went to the barbecue, Liam turned up, then Harper. There was an argument. Liam stayed in my saloon for the night, and he'd left by morning.

"What time did he leave?"

"I don't know. I didn't check the time. I felt the boat rock during the night. Oh, no! That might have been Harper getting in the well-deck!"

"What's a well-deck?"

"The bit at the front of a narrowboat—where Harper was."

She made a note, and then asked, "You didn't hear anything else? A thump, or anything?"

"No, I slept badly, but when I did get to sleep, it must have been heavily."

"Why did Liam leave?"

"I didn't want him to stay in the first place—but he'd drunk too much to drive. I told him to sleep in his car. In the end, I gave in and put him up in the saloon. He left me a note before he went."

"Have you got it?"

"I threw it away. It's in the bin on the boat."

"That's fine. Forensics will find it."

She asked me to ring Liam. I did, but there was no reply. She'd told me not to leave a message. I cancelled the call and explained that he was in the habit of turning his phone off when driving. I told her all I could about his car, but I couldn't remember the make

[46]

or registration, or even where he was living, so I gave her his parent's address.

"How did he seem when he joined you on the boat? After the incident outside?"

"I—I don't know."

"He was angry," said Freda. "He was wound up and angry at Harper."

I looked at Freda.

"Well, that's how he seemed to me, lass. You were a bit upset yourself."

"Madison, how would you describe Liam's character?" asked the DS.

"What? You think he killed Harper?" I laughed, and then checked myself—this was no joke.

"Madison?" She wasn't laughing.

"Er, well. He's serious. He can be kind, but if he is, there's usually an ulterior motive, so I suppose at heart he's selfish."

"Does he have a temper?"

"Well, yes. We all do."

"You know what I mean."

"He can get angry quickly."

"What does he do when he's angry?"

"Yells and shouts."

"He doesn't lose control?"

[47]

"He can get very—er—animated, I guess."

"Has he ever hit you?"

I shuffled in my seat and looked around the boat.

"Madison?"

"He's pushed me a couple of times. The last time was when I had the accident."

"Has he ever hit you?" she repeated gently.

I blinked away tears which were welling up. Freda put her hand on my arm.

"A couple of times, but I hit him once, too," I mumbled.

"He was angry at you?"

I nodded. "It was my fault, though."

The first time, I'd wound him up, and he'd hit me in the stomach. It was harder than he meant to, but it took me by surprise, which made it worse. The second time, I thought he was going to hit me, so I slapped him first, and he retaliated— a knee jerk reaction. I think I passed out briefly. He was so apologetic afterwards. I felt sorry for him.

"Did you report these incidents to the police?"

I shook my head.

After the DS left, Freda made coffee. I was afraid we were going to sit in awkward silence, or that she would ask me questions or try to comfort me, but she sat, held my hand, and switched on the TV. After an hour or so, Carlton turned up, by then I was feeling better.

"Are you allowed to talk to us?" Freda asked him.

"Not about last night, the detective said—but she knows as well as we do, that's not going to happen."

"So what went on after Freda and I left?" I asked.

"Not much. We were on the verge of a punch up, but Adam, and your guy, Liam, managed to bring us down a notch. Harper went back to his boat. Then I helped Adam clear up the barbecue stuff."

"Liam said you were arguing about something else?"

"What he did to you Madison—bang out of order. I know you shouldn't speak ill of the dead, but I never liked the guy."

A short while later, Jill and Adam joined us. It seemed that everyone wanted to check on me and talk over what had happened. After a catch-up, during which we learned nothing new, Freda started to put together some lunch for us all. I went out to stretch my legs. I'd forgotten my pain killers, and I wanted to ask the DS if someone could get them.

The police had cordoned off both my boat and Harper's. There were still a lot of people in white cover-alls wandering around. It didn't look as if they were going to finish anytime soon. I found the DS. After a friendly chastisement for not getting my meds earlier, she told me that I probably wouldn't be able to go back onto Mercury for a couple of days.

"Where will you go?" she asked.

"No idea," I replied.

"I can help you there," said a voice from behind me. "I'm Danny Stowell. My wife and I run the B&B." He pointed up to the house. "We've a couple of spare rooms that are aren't booked until the weekend. You're welcome to use one—free of charge under the circumstances."

I was so relieved at his offer. Arrangements were made, and I gave the DS a list of things I needed.

"Am I a suspect?" I couldn't help asking her.

She pursed her lips.

"Everyone's a suspect, Madison. He was found on your boat, which in some ways makes you less of one."

"Rule nothing in and nothing out?" I said.

"That's about the size of it."

When Freda heard that I wasn't allowed back on the boat, she offered me a bed with her on Bradford Bell, but I gracefully declined and explained that it was all sorted. It was kind of her, but I wasn't in the mood to share. In truth, I could do with my own space— lovely as Freda was. I asked if she could look after Ember. She had looked after her before and was delighted to help.

Late in the afternoon, the DS came back.

"You're free to go, but don't leave the area."

"I've no plans to," I said.

"Your stuff's been taken to the B&B, except these," she held up Ember's food and pointed to a bag of litter and her litter tray which were sitting on the bank with her cat bed.

I took the cat food and handed it to Freda.

"I'll do your statements tomorrow. There are other things I need to attend to now." She turned to go, then hesitated and turned back. "You realise there will be an inquest. You'll most likely be asked to give evidence".

Freda and I looked at each other.

Once the DS had gone, an oppressive gloom hung over us all. We talked a little, particularly about having to give evidence, which we dreaded. I decided to say my goodbyes and headed up to the house. As I got to the gate, the DS called out to me. She was heading up from my boat. I stopped and waited while she caught me up.

"What is it?" I asked.

"The note Liam left you, what did it say?"

"I can't remember exactly. He said he still loved me and he realised that my accident had affected my thinking or something like that."

"The first bit, about last night."

I thought.

"I don't know. I didn't read it properly. I was too relieved he'd gone to care."

She held up a plastic bag. It had the word 'Evidence' written on it. Inside was the note from Liam that forensics had recovered from my bin.

I looked at her, puzzled.

Without taking it out of the bag, I read it, but I only got to the end of the first part:

My lovely Madison.

It seems that I turned up at the right time. What that obnoxious bastard did to you is unforgivable. People like that shouldn't be allowed to live ...

I looked up at her, horrified.

"As soon as we've traced him", she said, "he'll be arrested on suspicion of murder."

Chapter 8

What a relief—to close my door and shut the world out.

I sat on the bed at the B&B in a haze, trying to process all that had happened. I couldn't believe Liam was a suspect. I knew he was a jerk, but still.

I looked around. What a contrast to Mercury. By comparison, it felt so large, there was room to swing a cat—sorry Ember. There were twin beds, with matching linen. I bounced up and down where I sat, then lay down. Snuggly. Nice.

There was a TV, a kettle, and the bits and pieces needed to make drinks—small packets of tea, coffee, that sort of thing. Oh, and an en-suite, how lovely. Showering on a narrowboat is fine, but nothing compared to a proper shower—and wow oh wow—a bath! It called out to me, enticing me in, promising great wonders. I succumbed.

The bath was simply marvellous. As I soaked and relaxed, all the tensions and stresses dissolved in the water. It was strange, washing my hair with my new haircut, but afterwards, I felt so much better. It's funny how a bath, washing your hair, stuff like that, changes your outlook on life. I felt fresh and reinvigorated.

Back in the bedroom, as I dried, I took in the view. My room was on the first floor at the back of the house. The window faced away from the canal and overlooked the track that must lead up to the long barrow. It was tree-lined and soon disappeared over a ridge. Someone had used a lot of poetic license when they called the place Barrow View. You would have to stand on the roof to see it. I wanted to take a walk up there some time and see what all the

[53]

fuss was all about. If I took it steady, my leg should be able to cope.

By the time I was dry and dressed, and had pottered about putting things away and tidying up, I was feeling hungry. There was a menu card on the dresser. I read through the options. It looked like Carlton was pretty handy in the kitchen. My tummy rumbled as I read. I was looking forward to finding out what he could do.

I headed out along the short corridor and down the stairs to the foyer. The dining room was on the right. It was larger than I expected. There were twenty tables, far more than needed to cater for the B&B. One of the leaflets in my room had explained that the restaurant was also open to the public. I gathered that it had a bit of a reputation locally.

A petite blonde greeted me as I entered the dining room. She smiled as I approached, and her deep blue eyes shone. She was a natural host and made me feel welcome before she had even spoken.

"Ah, you must be Madison," she beamed and held out a hand. "I'm Paula, Danny's wife."

"Lovely to meet you at last," I said. "I hope this is okay, staying here?"

"I'm glad he asked you. If he hadn't, I would have. It's all been such a shock, and so sad about Harper."

As she spoke, I glanced around the restaurant. It was almost empty.

"It won't be busy this evening, " Paula explained. "The police said we had to cancel the restaurant bookings. We're allowed to stay open for existing guests, though. It's only for today while they complete their enquiries, we're back to normal tomorrow. When will you be able to get back onto Mercury?"

"All being well, Friday."

"That'll be fine. We often get people in over the weekend to visit the long barrow, but it's been quiet since Easter."

"Oh, yes, the long barrow. I was hoping to go up there tomorrow."

"It's well worth a visit." Then she added as an afterthought, "There will be no bill for anything during your stay. It's the least we can do after the shock you've had."

"I'm grateful but—"

She held up her hand to stop me speaking.

"Not up for discussion." She led me to a table where she introduced me to the other guests—she had grouped us all together. I was the last of eight. There was a family from Manchester—parents and a toddler, a young couple taking a late spring break, and two older ladies, Eliza and June, who had come specifically to visit the long barrow. When I realised all the guests would be eating at the same table, I had a moment of panic. I wasn't in the mood for chit chat, not after recent events.

Paula explained to us that although the full menu was available, there might be a slight delay in service, as she was the only server that night.

"Everything is cooked from scratch by our own brilliant chef, who has experience from over the world." She winked surreptitiously at me. She had omitted to point out that Carlton's international experience was as a rifleman, not a chef. I grinned and began to relax.

Paula's judgement about the shared table was perfect. It was the right thing to do. Conversation flowed and was easy. Of course, the main topic was the murder, and I was the star of the show. I had to admit that it did help to talk about it. Until then I'd only spoken to Freda and the police, so to relate everything that had happened to people I didn't know was strangely cathartic.

Eliza and June were excessively enthusiastic about an astronomical alignment at the barrow. Jupiter and Saturn had recently conjugated, which meant they'd lined up. The ladies eagerly explained, this only happened every twenty years or so. The day before yesterday, there was a direct alignment with the barrow entrance, and both stars were in the constellation of Gemini. Apparently, this is especially significant if your birth sign is Gemini, which mine is not.

The meal was amazing. I went for a spiced chickpea and spinach pie. I had to admit I was blown away. I had no idea how Carlton learned his trade, but he'd learned it damned well. Looking around the table at what he had produced for the others, he could easily cook in a fancy place in London. The other guests all felt the same. There were plenty of compliments flying around. Here was a guy they'd be mad to lose.

None of us could resist ordering dessert, and I innocently went for the cheesecake. Oh my Lord! By the time I'd finished, I'd decided that I had to marry Carlton. He was a genius. It was hard to understand why he worked here, in the middle of nowhere.

The family with the toddler left after dessert, at which point things got a lot quieter. After a decaf coffee and a liqueur nightcap, I was ready to head up to bed. My leg was aching, and I needed to lie down, but I hung back as I wanted to thank Carlton. Eventually, the two ladies and the young couple left, and I headed towards a door which I guessed was the kitchen. I knocked and opened it without waiting for a reply.

I walked in on Carlton and Paula engaged in a deep passionate kiss. They guiltily broke apart at my intrusion.

"Oh er, sorry—"

Damn—I won't be marrying Carlton after all. I stammered out a thank you for the excellent meal, retreated and headed upstairs.

Paula caught up with me as I reached the landing.

"I'm so sorry, Madison. You shouldn't have seen that."

"No, it's my fault. I wanted to thank Carlton."

"He is something else, isn't he? A real talent." She noticed I was juggling with my stick, bag and key, so she held out her hand for my key and unlocked the door for me.

"To tell the truth, Paula, it was amazing. Possibly the best meal I've ever had."

We went into my room, and I sat on the bed, stretching out my aching leg.

"Does it hurt much?" she asked. She was prevaricating and clearly wanted to talk.

"Comes and goes. It's more of an ache now, but it's always worse at the end of the day."

As I spoke, she sank onto the couch.

She was silent. I felt a need to fill the empty space.

"You don't need to say anything, " I said, "It's none of my business."

"I want to. I need to talk to someone."

Cathartic. I knew about that.

"Our marriage, me and Danny, it's terrible."

"From all I've heard, you seem so good together."

"Our public face is well-rehearsed. We've been married for fifteen years. It took him less than two years to get bored with me. I pretended not to know. I loved him. The second time he wandered, I had it out with him. He was repentant and begged me not to leave him. We decided to start afresh, sold up, gave up our jobs and bought this place. That was eight years ago," she sighed. "At first we were busy decorating, changing things, upgrading the rooms, so we just got on with it. While we were doing it, we had something in common—a shared purpose. But after things were sorted, it was obvious that we'd grown even further apart. He began to resent me—and now he's got nasty. He won't do anything in public, but he's not a nice man, and he's getting worse."

"Is he—?"

"Violent? Not to me. Not yet, at any rate. He rants and raves at me, about how I ruined his life—usually when he's been drinking, which is more and more these days."

"Is he seeing anyone?"

"Not that I know of. I don't know what he does—and honestly,

I wouldn't care if he did. In fact, I wish he would. It would probably give him something else to do apart from despising me. We've not slept together for years. He moved out of our room ages ago, thank goodness. I didn't miss him. But I did miss being with a man," she sighed.

Then she carried on, now with a spring in her voice. "Then Carlton came along. He was understanding and lovely." She looked up at me, her face beaming, "I fell for him, Madison. What began as purely physical—"

I got the picture.

"Does Danny know?"

"God, no! I think if he knew about Carlton, he'd kill him."

"That wouldn't be easy."

"No," she almost laughed and dabbed her damp eyes with her sleeve. "He tried to sack him, though, but for something else."

"Why? He's a genius."

"Danny used to do all the cooking. We only took Carlton on to help when we were converting the final three rooms upstairs. Danny's a good cook, but we quickly realised that Carlton's on another level, and he stole Danny's thunder. Word spread, and suddenly our restaurant was a destination. Danny wasn't the centre of attention any more—it was all about Carlton. That was before—"

I handed her a tissue, and she blew her nose.

"You won't tell anyone, will you?"

"Soul of discretion. But why are you both still here? Carlton could work anywhere."

"Because of me. We've spent years building this place up, and I'm not ready to walk away from it all—not yet, anyway—and Carlton refuses to leave without me."

After Paula had gone, I went to bed and lay mulling over what Paula had told me, but soon, inevitably, my thoughts returned to Liam and Harper. Could Liam have stabbed him? If he had, why? Liam could be vindictive and nasty, but was that enough? Did he see Harper as a threat? It made no sense. Was it a coincidence that Harper was found dead on Mercury, or had he been coming after Liam—or me? Surely if Liam had killed him, it would have been better if he'd gone back to bed after and feigned innocence, not run away—unless he panicked. And why would he murder Harper and then be stupid enough to leave a note with such a toxic threat?

No, it couldn't have been him. Liam must have got up, dressed, written the note, gathered his stuff and left.

Someone else knifed Harper, either on his boat or on the bank, after Liam left. So who was it?

It could have been anyone. It could have been an outside job.

And why did Harper end up on Mercury?

Questions seemed to endlessly march around my mind. Eventually, the events of the day overcame me, and I drifted off.

Chapter 9

The following morning I awoke after a surprisingly good night's sleep. I got up, showered and headed down to the dining room.

Breakfast was continental style: yoghurt, fruit, croissants, toast, that kind of thing. The young family were the only other guests in the restaurant. I spent breakfast smiling, waving and playing hide and seek behind the menu card with their outrageously cute toddler.

When I was finished, I headed down to the canal to find out when I could get the boat back. There was no-one around. The tape was still in place, around both boats, but there were no police or forensics.

"Hi, Madison," called Freda.

"Oh, hi." I headed over to her. "Seen anyone around?"

"Not this morning dear. Was it today they said you could go back on?"

"Yes, they said Friday, but they didn't say what time. I suppose I ought to wait until they say something."

"Well, come on in and wait, then. Let me make you a cup of tea."

It was nice to be back on her boat. It felt familiar and safe. We sat and chatted over all that had happened. She said the previous day forensics were gone by seven in the evening. With no sign of them today, maybe it boded well for getting back on Mercury later.

I enthused about Carlton's cooking. Freda had never eaten at the restaurant. She had heard he was good but had no idea he was that good. I wanted to ask her about Danny and Paula, and if she was aware of any problems they were having, but it felt a bit treacherous, so I said nothing.

I hung out with Freda for a couple of hours, and I was beginning to think I ought to leave her in peace, when there was knock on the door. It was DS Jackie Meade.

Freda invited her in with enthusiasm. She made coffee all around and broke out the homemade biscuits.

Jackie told me the bad news: I wasn't going to get the boat back until tomorrow.

"But there's nothing going on," I pointed out.

"I'm sorry. I'm only the messenger. It's out of my hands. They've taken all their samples, but until certain tests are complete, they don't want the site contaminated in case they need to come back. All being well it will be tomorrow morning. Is there anything else you need from the boat?"

"No, I'm well looked after at Barrow View."

"Do ye not have to vacate your room there?" Freda asked.

"They've got guests arriving tomorrow, but they won't be there until after lunch, so I'm good for tonight."

"The reason I came to find you, Madison, is that I need to take a formal statement, and fingerprints and a DNA sample for exclusion purposes. I would have done it yesterday, Liam was arrested, and I led the interview."

[62]

"Are you charging him?"

"No. It's highly likely my DI will release him later today on police bail. He remains a person of interest for the time being. To be honest, we're coming to the conclusion the murder was drug-related. It seems Harper was both a junkie and a pusher, and things went wrong."

"He was into drugs?"

"I can't say too much, but seems he was lying low."

"Why here?" I asked.

She shrugged. "There must be some connection. We may know more once I've seen all the statements. When did he first turn up?" Jackie looked at Freda.

"Nae long. Two or three months. I dinnae ken."

"Where did he come from?" Jackie asked.

"Dinnae ken. Danny or Paula may be able to tell you more. They may have talked to him. But, er—"

"I'm talking to Paula later," interrupted Jackie. "Now, is there somewhere we can go, Madison?"

"Oh, dinnae fash, lass," Freda said. "I need to get some shopping. You stay here. Make yourselves at home."

I made us both coffee. Jackie took my fingerprints and a DNA swab. I confirmed that I'd never been on Harper's boat, or even touched it. She got out a statement pad, and I went over what had happened again, while she wrote it down. It was all a recapitulation of what I had said before. I couldn't think of anything else of

[63]

significance. I signed at the bottom of each sheet.

She got up and started to gather her things, "I'll be back later to talk to Freda. I'm off to find Paula."

"Have you spoken to Danny yet?"

"He's Paula's husband, isn't he? Yes, one of my colleagues did yesterday. I've read his statement. Nothing of interest. It's a lovely set up they've got. Not sure I could work with my husband as happily as they do. We'd be arguing within a week!" She grinned at me, but slowly her smile faded as she looked at me. I was trying to appear innocent but clearly failing.

"What do you know?" she asked, sitting down again. Darn, she was good.

"Nothing," I shifted uncomfortably.

"Spill."

"No, nothing to do with this."

She stared at me. "This isn't a negotiation; it's a murder enquiry. What do you know?"

I said nothing and took out my phone.

She scoffed and leaned back in her seat. "Okay, let's see where this game goes. It'll all come out in the inquest anyway. I have something new for you. We think Harper took some sleeping pills before the barbecue."

"I thought he was drunk or something—as I said in my statement."

"There was a lot of vodka on the boat. He might have started early with both—the booze and the pills—so by the time someone got on his boat, he would've been pretty woozy. He wouldn't have been up to defending himself. After they stabbed him he was still alive, and presumably tried to get to you for help—and that's how he ended up on your well-deck, sometime between two and two-thirty. Liam said he drove away soon after one in the morning."

"Why would someone stab him and not leave him dead?"

"I don't know. Maybe they didn't want to kill him, or thought he was dead." Jackie was getting irritated. "Now what have you got?"

I was uncomfortable betraying Paula's confidence. I took a sip of coffee. I had to say something.

"This didn't come from me. When you talk to Paula, throw in a question about their marriage."

"Oh? Why is that of interest?"

"It may not be. You could be right, and it was an outside job, but if not, every little thing helps."

"Okay, thanks." She paused, and then, "Madison if you hear—"

I pursed my lips and looked at her.

She nodded and left.

Chapter 10

After Jackie left, I phoned Freda and asked if she could pick me up something for lunch. She told me not to be so silly and to make myself something with whatever I could find on her boat. I had a hunt around and put together a pretty decent sandwich.

Halfway through my lunch, I decided to ring Isla. I thought I'd better update her on what was going on. Then I thought better of it and started a text, but no sooner had I started than I changed my mind. There was nothing she could do, other than worry. It might be better to wait.

After lunch, I decided not to wait for Freda to come back. I wanted to head back to my room at the house, maybe read and chill out. To be honest, I was at a bit of loose end and felt restless. Had I known I wasn't going to get back on the boat today, I might have taken a walk up to the long barrow, but it was the afternoon now, and I couldn't be bothered.

Back at the house, there was no-one around.

I went into the restaurant and looked out at the view. The windows faced the same direction as my room. There was a bird table set up, and I watched as it was laid siege to by enthusiastic late lunchers. It was a good turnout. There were sparrows, blue tits, great tits, and wagtails. Pigeons and blackbirds sauntered and hopped around on the ground, clearing up dropped seeds from the feeders.

I heard a noise in the kitchen and wondered if it was Paula. I went to have a look. It was Carlton.

"Oh, hi," I said.

"Hi, Madison."

"What brings you up here? Shouldn't you be enjoying your time off?"

"I wanted to check the kitchen is ready for this evening and do some prep. We're opening to the public again tonight. Did you enjoy your meal last night?"

"Carlton, it was stunning."

He looked embarrassed.

"That's kind. I do what I can."

"I'm not kidding. Where did you learn to cook like that?"

"Mum and Dad ran a restaurant, and I paid attention. Both of them were brilliant chefs. By the time I was ten, some of my ideas were getting on the menu. I loved cooking, and I loved helping out in their kitchen."

"Junior Masterchef material. Where did you train?"

"I didn't. My parents were killed in a car accident when I was fifteen."

"Oh! I'm so sorry."

"It was a long time ago. Anyway, I lost the will to cook. As soon as I could, I joined the army. Did twelve years standing around waiting to shoot people."

I smiled thinly.

"By the time I was due to leave, I was ready to cook again. As part of my severance package, I signed up on every culinary course

[67]

and restaurant management programme the army allowed. This is my first job, so I haven't had any proper kitchen experience."

"You could easily get a job in London now."

"I know, but—I'm happy here. My final tour of Iraq was bad. I like the peace."

"If they're paying you well, I guess that helps."

He laughed. "I'm definitely not here for the money. Although to be fair, I get a free mooring for the boat. That helps."

"And you have other things to stay for," I smiled.

He nodded.

"Do you love her?"

"I do, Madison." He looked me in the eye. He was serious. "It started off as a pleasant distraction but—"

I got the picture.

"But Danny doesn't know," I said.

"We both want to keep things quiet for the moment. Danny's a complete bastard, but she's too loyal for her own good. He's cheated on her more than once. If he hadn't done that, she wouldn't have given me a second look. The problem is what to do next. She doesn't want to walk out, not yet. Not if there's a chance she can keep this place."

He leaned against the counter and looked down at the floor.

"I do love her Madison," he said again, "and she—erm—"

"Yes, she told me," I said, thinking back to how her face lit up when she spoke about Carlton.

His eyes brightened.

"She did?" He laughed. "It was a hell of a shock to me, I can tell you. Was she happy? When she told you?"

"I would say so. She has a future to look forward to." Hmmm, that was an odd comment, I thought.

"I'm so glad." He turned back to the chopping board. "I'm sorry she's not told me yet, but I guess in her own good time."

"In her own good time," I mumbled as I watched him dice an onion. Had I missed something?

"I guess it'll be due in the new—" He froze and looked at me horrified. "That's not what you meant, is it?"

"What?" I asked.

"What I said."

"What did you say?"

He went back to chopping—then the penny dropped.

"Oh, she's expecting," I said brightly.

"Shh!" He dropped his knife on the worktop with a clatter. I glanced down as he laid a restraining hand on my arm. I noticed his knuckles were scraped. I was about to comment when he squeezed my arm gently. I looked up. My eyes met his, staring back at me anxiously.

"Please," he said, "she's kept it very quiet. I mean, very!"

"I won't tell anyone. That's wonderful news," I grinned. The obvious question about parentage flitted through my mind, but Paula had been adamant she hadn't slept with Danny for some time.

"What will you do?" I asked, instead.

He picked up his knife and carried on chopping.

"I don't know. It's early days." He stopped again. He looked nervous. "Please, keep it to yourself."

"Of course, I will. Don't worry." I threw him my most reassuring smile. I'm not sure it helped.

He stopped working again and looked at me and leaned closer to whisper in a confidential way.

"Don't even let—"

"Ah, there you are." DS Meade was at the door. "Can I have a word, Madison?" She indicated she wanted me to follow and headed off towards the restaurant.

"Don't worry, Carlton." I put a reassuring hand on his arm and went after her.

The DS was waiting for me.

"I'm done with Paula."

"Tell you anything interesting?"

"Nothing. Not even about Danny. As far as she's concerned, it's all good—which is what Danny said, too."

"Oh."

"But I didn't press her. She wasn't going to talk."

"Thanks."

"I didn't do it for your benefit. I don't mind if people sit and tell me irrelevant trivia, but I get pissed off when they tell me crap."

"I told you what she said to me."

"Not you—Paula and Danny. Something's going on. Maybe it is just their marriage. I could take them down the station for formal questioning, only to find out it's a waste of everyone's time. Or you can find out for me."

"I'll help where I can."

"I need you to help where you can't too. I'll let you know who I want you to talk to, once I've been through all the statements."

"I'm not sure I'm keen on spying for you."

"Madison, wake up! This is a murder enquiry. You won't be spying. You only need to point me in the right direction when something doesn't add up."

"Why me?"

"They're a tight bunch. You're an outsider, but they seem to talk to you."

She was right, and I'd noticed this before. Often, for some reason, people trust me and tell me things they won't tell others. I didn't want to betray anyone's confidences, but on the other hand, Jackie was right, a man had been killed.

"I'll see what I can do, but I can't promise anything."

"Good." Her tone reverted to detached professional. "I'm finished here for now. DNA and fingerprints results are being rushed through. They might throw up something. The only good thing about Harper being such a creep is that only a couple of people went on his boat—which narrows down the exclusion prints and DNA."

"From what I've heard, I'm surprised anyone went near him."

"I know what you mean. Obviously, Jill and Adam did, but Freda did too. She took him some biscuits, not long after he first arrived. Apparently, he wasn't into 'sweetmeats'. She got a bit upset. She said he swore at her."

"Poor Freda. But Jill and Adam? Why 'obviously'?"

"Oh!" She looked at me. "Are you saying that I know something you don't?"

"I don't know. Do you?"

"No, no," she held a hand up and closed her eyes.

"What?"

"Let me gloat for a few moments—please."

"Should I wait in the hall?"

She laughed.

"You didn't know Harper's boat is owned by Jill and Adam?"

I shook my head. I certainly didn't.

Chapter 11

I headed upstairs to my room. I'd spent two months in hospital either lying down or sitting down, so understandably I was finding all the walking and standing around tiring. My leg was aching more than ever. I could handle that, but now my brain was beginning to suffer from overload too. All I'd done in hospital was listen to the radio and watch a bit of TV. There was interaction with other patients and staff, but that was limited, and if I was lucky, someone turned up to visit me. To be fair, I'd had plenty of visitors, but with the best will in the world, visitors are only around for a few hours a week. Now, suddenly I was out in the big wide world, with all this going on.

"Madison."

I looked around. Paula was coming up the stairs after me.

"Have the police gone?" she asked.

"Yes. Did you speak to the DS?"

She nodded.

"Come on," I said.

We went into my room, and I asked if she could make us a cup of tea. I needed to stop moving around. I sat on the bed and put my leg up.

"I like this room," I said.

"It was one of the first we re-modelled. It was so exciting when we first took over. The place was so run down—it hadn't seen a lick of paint for years. There were no moorings. We had the electricity and water run down so we could set them up. They were our main source of income for the first few years. Did you know we own Auf Wiedersehen?"

"The boat at the end? Yes, Freda said."

"We got it a few years ago as an attempt to help our marriage. It was my idea. We went out cruising a couple of times, but it didn't work. Once we're out of the public gaze, it all falls apart."

"Are you going to sell it?"

"We've rented it out a couple of times. Not for people to go off cruising, more as extra accommodation. It's worked pretty well. I want to make it more official and let people hire it out properly, for cruising holidays. Danny doesn't. He thinks we should sell it to get the regular income from the mooring."

She handed me a cup of tea.

"Thanks. I guess there are arguments both ways. Letting the boat out would be more money, but more hassle."

"To be honest, the real reason I wanted to keep it was to use as a bolt-hole if I needed one. Then Carlton came along."

"Is it right that Jill and Adam own Harper's boat?"

"Yes. There was a man moored there about a year ago. When he left, we were going to advertise the mooring, but then Adam asked if he could take it as he was planning to buy a second boat for his sister."

"That's nice of him."

"Adam asked for a discount, as he'd be renting out two slots. I was fine with it, but Danny wasn't. He reckoned Adam was already getting the moorings cheap. If we put it up for auction, there would be a lot of interest—it's such a great location."

"But you talked Danny into letting Adam have it?"

"Didn't need to in the end. Adam spun a tale about some problems his sister was having, then he changed his tune and offered us top dollar. I got the impression he would have paid whatever we asked. Then maybe three months ago, he bought Red Rum and moored her up there."

"So if Adam bought it for his sister, it's her boat?" I could see that a conversation with Jill or Adam was on the cards.

"I don't know who owns it, but it's registered in Adam's name. As part of the mooring contract, we get copies of the boat licence which is registered with the Canal and River Trust and the insurance. Both are in his name."

"When did she leave, then?"

"Oh, erm—" she hesitated, "she's—she never arrived." She seemed a bit cagey. Was there something else?

"So how come Harper ended up there?"

"A couple of months ago, he turned up out of the blue and moved in. I noticed his motorbike first—it's still out in the car park. Danny went to see him one day. Apparently, Harper was very rude and told him to speak to Adam. I know you shouldn't speak ill of the dead, but I never liked the man."

"Funny, Carlton said the same thing."

"There's no love lost there. Harper was into drugs, Carlton hates anything to do with them. He says he saw too much of it in the army."

"After the rumpus last night, Liam seemed to think there was something else going on between them."

"Rumpus?" she laughed. "Not heard that word for a while. I don't know. Carlton did seem to be more angry at Harper recently—maybe it was my imagination?"

"Hmm."

"Anyway, when Danny spoke to Adam after Harper had blown him off, Adam was all apologetic. It turned out that Harper was his sister's boyfriend. She was abroad and was meant to be joining Harper when she got back. Adam assumed Harper would've introduced himself to Danny when he arrived."

"She's his girlfriend? Poor girl. Has she been told what happened?"

"No idea. We've got no details for her. I presume Adam has though, and that he's been in touch."

I mulled over what she had told me. She was sitting on the sofa and seemed relaxed and chatty. I thought it might be a good time to see if I could get any background on her and Danny.

"What did you do? Before all of this?"

She smiled. "I was an events manager. That's where I met Danny."

"Oh?"

"I arranged corporate team-building events. High-end ones. Not your quad bike racing or stuff like that. More like week-long hiking in Norway."

"Oh, wow!"

"It certainly was wow. It was an amazing job. I got to travel around the world to assess locations and activities. During the events, I provided on-site support to clients. It was such fun!" She visibly brightened up as she reminisced. "I got to join in too. Any problems, all I had to do was hassle the locations to sort them, but I was good at my job, so usually things went brilliantly."

"Of course."

"And I got to meet a load of hot guys, who were, shall we say, prepared for all sorts of things."

"Extra-curricular activity," I grinned.

"That's how I met Danny. He was such fun. Had a wicked sense of humour. We got on from the moment we met, and we were married within a year."

"You were both unattached?"

"I was, and he had recently gone through his second divorce. Maybe I should have read that as a sign and been more cautious, but his charm blew me away. Things were great for almost two years."

"Then, he wandered."

"Hmm."

"What was his job?"

"He was a senior comms engineer. At the time his company was at the forefront of rolling out the 4G mobile network. They were on a junket in Italy."

"Nice. So if I get a problem with my phone—"

"Ha, yes." She sipped her tea and changed the subject. "Have you been up to the long barrow yet? You said you wanted to go."

"I was going today, but I never got around to it."

"If you fancy it tomorrow?"

"I certainly would. Morning's good for me. How long will it take?"

"At your speed? Half an hour."

"At my speed!" I laughed.

"Sorry, you know what I mean."

"No, that's okay, you've got a point. To be honest, I was a bit reluctant to go on my own—in case I got stranded, but I'm sure I'll be fine."

"It's not far. Let's say, ten o'clock?"

"Ten o'clock it is."

Chapter 12

The weather forecast on my phone app assured me it would be dry all day, so I shoved a rain mac into my backpack. This is England, after all.

Paula texted me to check that our expedition was still on. She said she would join me at reception.

I was downstairs soon after ten. I didn't have to wait long, and we headed off.

"Do you want me to carry your backpack?" she asked.

"No, I'm fine thanks. As long as I use my stick, it's all good. If I put too much weight on my leg, I get a nasty twinge that hurts like hell. If we go slow, I'll be fine."

We went up the track that ran alongside the house. It turned away from the canal and rose gently towards the woods which were set on a slope. Paula was patient and kept down to my pace. I was frustrated but had to accept my lot. If I tried to go too fast, I knew it wouldn't end well.

"This will be the longest I've walked since the accident," I said.

"Well, there's no rush. It's not all that far. The long barrow is around five thousand years old—it's not going anywhere."

Soon we reached the trees, where the track began to climb.

"Was it a burial chamber?" I said.

"Nobody's sure. The remains of two people were discovered there when it was excavated, but no other remains. There's a main chamber, and a series of smaller side chambers, all with stone supports. It looks as if it was altered more than once, but no other human bones have been found, and there was none of the usual evidence suggesting it was used for burials. If it wasn't, then it's anyone's guess as to what it was used for, but it must have taken some effort to create it in the first place."

"Ha," I laughed. "You sound like Carlton, an archaeology nerd on the quiet."

She smiled.

We regularly paused for a few moments, so I could give my leg a rest. It wasn't hurting, but I didn't want to overdo it. The woods were marvellous. It had rained overnight, so it was fresh and smelt of earth and wood. The birds were singing, and occasionally squirrels chased around high up in the branches. We met a group of hikers making their way back down the track, but other than that it was surprisingly quiet.

We chatted as we walked. I wanted to find a way to ask about what Carlton had told me, but I didn't want to sound nosy.

"What are you going to do?" asked Paula, "when Isla comes back?"

"In spite of all that's happened, I love the boat. The minimalist life, simple and off-grid, appeals to me at the moment. I'm seriously thinking of buying my own. I haven't got anywhere I can call home, so if I get a boat, I could go off cruising and try to concentrate on finishing my dissertation."

"Sounds appealing."

The path through the woods became steeper than I expected. Looking from Barrow View, I hadn't appreciated the lay of the land or realised that we would head upwards so quickly. Then we broke out on the other side of the trees, and there was the barrow. From this side, it looked like an elongated grass mound at the top of the hill.

"Ooo, there's the entrance," I said. At the end of the mound to my right were some small standing stones. I headed towards them, but when I got there, I found a neat stone wall with the mound above. I was expecting a door, but there was nothing. I turned and saw that Paula was grinning at me.

"That's the false doorway," she explained. "They were used to confuse thieves. Carry on round to the other side."

As I passed the false door, I was greeted by a stunning view. The land opened up and fell away down to a valley.

"I had no idea we had gone up so high. Look, there's the canal!" I gasped. The glittering moss green ribbon of the canal struck out across the valley. I couldn't see Ducks in a Row, as it was hidden around the corner of the hill which we had walked up.

"It's some view isn't it," Paula said.

"Amazing."

We made our way around and found a small doorway, the real entrance.

I went to head in, but Paula placed a hand on my shoulder.

"Wait. Look."

I wasn't sure what I was looking for, but then a bird appeared in the air near the entrance, flittered around and disappeared inside.

"A swallow?" I said as I looked up into the sky for more.

"Swift."

"I always get them mixed up."

"They nest inside the barrow most years. I was up here the other day and saw they were back."

"Don't they mind the visitors?"

"Don't seem to—they keep coming back. Wait a moment."

After no more than a minute the bird skipped out, so quickly that if I had blinked, I'd have missed it.

"Wow, amazing," I laughed.

"They usually set up in one of the side chambers inside the door. Come on, let's go in before she comes back."

We went inside. I stood and blinked, trying to get accustomed to the darkness. Paula put a finger to her lips and pointed to the entrance. We both fell silent, and after a moment, the swift appeared and shot straight into a chamber on the left. It was so fast I could hardly see it. How it managed to control its speed in such a small space, I have no idea. We stood and waited. A minute later, it was out and gone.

We beamed at each other—it was magical.

I took a look around. It was dark and gloomy, but Paula had brought a torch. The main chamber was around thirty meters long and in places two meters wide, with six side chambers of various sizes. The largest side chamber was sort of round, with about eight or nine square meters of floor. The walls were made of a mix of stones of every size. Some were small brick-like stones, and the largest were as tall as two meters, all built like dry stone walling. Paula pointed out nooks built into the wall, possibly for placing lamps.

After looking around, we went back out into the light. There was a bench nearby. We sat and gazed at the view. Clouds were rolling in from the west, casting shadows over the fields below.

I felt spots of rain. I got my mac out of my backpack. I knew the weather app was not to be trusted.

"How's your leg?" asked Paula.

"Surprisingly, not bad at all. Taking it slow worked well. I'll be so glad when it's back to normal. I used to love running, and I'm missing it. Never mind about me though, what about you?"

"I'm fine. Why? What do you mean?"

I tried not to be a bull in a china shop.

"Well, you know—" I prompted.

She looked at me blankly, and I decided not to pry further.

"Shall we head back now?" I asked. "Join me for lunch on the boat?"

"Sounds good."

We got up and started back around the barrow.

"What did you mean? About how I am?" she asked.

"A little bird told me—" I smiled.

Her face fell, and she stopped walking.

"Madison, what have you heard?" She sounded stern.

[83]

"Gossip," I lied. "I heard you were expecting."

"Expecting!" Her hand flew to her mouth as she stifled a gasp. She turned away, and I thought she might be composing herself, but when she turned back, she looked like thunder.

"Whose gossip?"

"I was talking to Carlton," I said as cheerfully as I could. I wished I hadn't said anything.

"Carlton? Don't make me laugh! You've been talking to Danny!" She was angry.

"Danny? I've hardly passed the time of day with him."

"Don't freaking lie to me. You bitch!" She stormed. "You freaking bitch! Danny sent you up here!"

"What?" I was dumbstruck.

Then my phone rang.

"He's sent you to snoop!" she was shouting.

"No!" I yelled back as I managed to get my phone from my pocket.

"I'd expect him to do such a low thing—but you!"

"No, Paula!" What the hell was she on about?

The call was from the DS. I'd better take it.

"Find your own freaking way back," Paula shouted as she stormed off.

"Hello?" I said into the phone. I was still flustered.

"Hi, Madison. Forensics are done with your boat, but Harper's is still off-limits. Go back whenever you like. You can move the tape out of the way."

"Oh good," I said. I watched Paula striding down the hill towards the woods. I tried to hobble after her while juggling with my stick and phone.

"Also," Jackie said, "as I hoped, the forensics results have changed everything. Madison, we've found the killer at last!"

"That's great," I said.

I listened as she updated me. I couldn't believe what she was saying.

I rang off.

"Paula, wait!" I yelled.

"Piss off!" she threw over her shoulder.

"Wait, Paula—they've arrested Carlton! They're going to charge him with murder!"

Chapter 13

We didn't talk in the car.

After the phone call at the barrow, I'd told Paula I would go back to the boat, but, to my surprise, after all she had said, she wanted me with her for moral support. I think she'd also picked up that the DS and I were on good terms, and she probably hoped that might help.

We pulled up at the police station and went in.

"I'm here to see Carlton Embry," she said to the desk sergeant, a little curtly I thought.

"I'm sorry madam, he is not allowed visitors—and you are?"

"But I must see him—"

"Paula," I interrupted and guided her away from the desk. "If he's not been charged yet and is still being questioned, you won't be allowed to see him. I'll see if I can get Jackie to talk to us."

I turned back to the desk.

"My apologies. Could I speak to DS Jackie Meade, please? Could you tell her it's Madison Leigh and Paula Stowell."

The sergeant appeared a little more amenable and picked up a phone. After a brief discussion, he hung up.

"If you'd like to take a seat, she'll be along shortly."

We took a seat. 'Shortly' turned out to be nearly fifty minutes of awkward silence between us. She didn't seem inclined to talk, and although I wanted to say something, I decided I'd better hold my peace for the moment.

Eventually, Jackie appeared at a door to the side of the sergeant's desk. "Could you come this way please."

We followed, and she led us down a short corridor and through a door on the left. We were in an interview room. We all sat down.

"Sorry to keep you. It's been hectic this afternoon," she said. "I'm sorry you can't see Carlton. We will be interviewing him again in the morning, after which we will make a decision about a referral to the CPS."

"The CPS?" asked Paula.

"The Crown Prosecution Service. They will look at the evidence and decide whether or not he should be prosecuted."

Paula gasped. "Surely he's allowed to see someone?"

"He had a solicitor present during the interview earlier, but until we decide what to do, no, I'm afraid not. But I'm glad you came along Mrs Stowell—"

The door opened.

"Gov?" A uniformed constable put his head in the room.

"Yes, we're ready," Jackie said to him.

He came in and sat on the vacant chair next to the Detective Sargeant. He took out the now-familiar statement pad and a pen.

Paula was about to say something and then changed her mind.

The DS frowned at Paula. "When I took your statement, you told me that on Wednesday 16th April, after the restaurant closed, you went up to bed and spent the night on your own." She paused and gave Paula a loaded look. "Would you like the opportunity to add anything?"

Paula glanced at me, then looked down at her hands.

Jackie spoke again. "You don't have to say anything, of course. But then I will have to consider whether to arrest you for obstructing a police investigation and making a false statement. Then we can do all this again with you under caution and a solicitor present."

After a moment Paula replied with a dejected, but simple, "Okay".

The DS nodded to the constable indicating that he should fill in the interview paperwork with the date, time, and a list of those present. I was expecting to be asked to leave, but Jackie directed him to add my name to the list.

Jackie began the interview.

"Mrs Stowell you have said that you would like to comment further regarding the statement you made on Friday, April 18th.

There was a pause, and Paula spoke.

"In my statement, I said I spent the night alone. That wasn't true. As I said previously, that evening was Carlton's night off, so Danny did the cooking, I worked front of house, and we had a waiter and waitress working the tables. It was quiet that evening, so I let the staff leave early, around nine forty-five. I oversaw the final customers—they were gone soon after ten—then I cleared up in the restaurant. Danny finished closing down the kitchen and went upstairs about ten-thirty. Then I set up ready for breakfast— I was done by eleven. I sent a text to Carlton, to let him know the coast was clear. We're—having an affair."

"How long?" Jackie asked.

"A few months—Danny and I have been sleeping apart for years after he cheated on me. Then I went up to my room. A bit later Carlton let himself in. He has his own key."

"Did he tell you about anything that had happened earlier that evening?"

"He said there had been a barbecue at Ducks in a Row. That's the moorings," she added for the benefit of the constable who was writing everything down. "He said Madison's ex-boyfriend had turned up—he said his name, but I can't remember it— and later Harper came out and caused a scene."

"Did he say anything more specific about this 'scene'?"

"He said Harper assaulted Madison, and she was shaken up."

"Was that all he said?"

"About what happened at the barbecue?" she looked up puzzled.

"Yes. Did Carlton say anything else about Harper?"

Paula sat, looking at her hands again and said nothing.

"Mrs Stowell?" said Jackie gently.

"He said he hated Harper."

"Was that all?"

"He went on about how he hated Harper and hated drugs. When he was young, he had a friend who died of an overdose, and in the army—" her voice trailed away.

[89]

Jackie spoke up. "He was dishonourably discharged after assaulting an Iraqi civilian. It's a matter of record, Mrs Stowell."

"Yes, except he had a good reason. The guy he was accused of assaulting was pushing drugs to British soldiers in the compound in Basra and using local kids as drugs mules. And the guy pulled a knife on him."

"The point is, he has an assault on his record."

"He's not like that. He's not a violent man."

"Well clearly he is, but let's move on." Jackie thought for a moment and then asked, "How did he seem when he was telling you about the barbecue?"

"He was—," she paused.

"Angry?" suggested the DS.

"Jackie!" I said, "Maybe we do need a solicitor here?"

She put up her hands.

"Sorry. Please answer the question in your own words."

"Not angry." She thought for a moment. "He was hyped up—excitable. I calmed him down, and he was fine."

"Did he say anything else about Harper?"

Paula sighed.

"That he was a bas—"

She stopped talking and looked at me and then the DS.

Jackie said, "We're all adults here, Mrs Stowell."

"He said Harper was an effing bastard. Except he didn't say

'effing' and I'm not going to repeat what he did say."

"Anything else?"

"He went on about how he was a low life drug pusher, and it was his fault that Sonia died."

"Sonia?" I said.

"Adam's sister," Paula said.

"She's dead? How did—" I paused as Jackie put up her hand, reminding me that she was asking the questions.

"Go on," Jackie said to Paula.

"Adam bought the boat for her—Red Rum. The one Harper uses. He was her boyfriend. I don't know much about it. You'd need to talk to Adam."

She repeated what she had told me about Adam's sister when we were talking in my room. The only difference was that previously she hadn't mentioned Sonia's name, or that she had died. No wonder I'd thought there was something she was holding back.

"What time did Carlton leave?" Jackie asked.

"I don't know, sometime in the night."

"Come on Mrs Stowell. You can do better than that. You've already wasted police time."

"After I calmed him down, we, er—. And then we fell asleep. I think it was about a quarter to two, maybe a bit later."

"Are you pregnant?"

Paula looked at her horrified, and then at me.

"Madison! What have you said?"

"Nothing!" I was as shocked at the question as Paula.

"I didn't find out from her," the DS said. "So are you?"

"No," she said, shaking her head vigorously.

"Why did Harper think that you were?"

"Harper? Harper thought I was—?" She held her hand to her mouth as she gasped.

"It's okay," I rested a hand on her shoulder.

She tried to pull herself together and explain. "Danny and I had a blazing row one night. He was boasting about—about—his affairs with other women, and saying horrible things," she stifled a sob, "so I just blurted it out. Then I added to the lie and said it wasn't his, although he would have realised that—we'd been sleeping separately for ages. I wanted to get back at him, to hurt him. I was grasping at straws, Madison."

"You told him it was Carlton's?" the DS asked.

"No, I would never do that! He doesn't know about Carlton. We've been so careful. How do you know Harper thought I was?"

"Would he tell Harper?" Jackie ignored her question.

"No! Danny didn't like Harper."

"Why?"

"I don't know. He wasn't a likeable person."

Paula went quiet as she thought, and then Jackie asked as if to clarify, "But you're not pregnant?"

Paula shook her head again. "No."

"Have you ever had sexual relations with Harper?"

"Good grief! No!" she was clearly upset that the question had even been asked.

After some final wrap up questions, Jackie seemed satisfied. She got Paula to read through the interview, and we all signed each page. She told Paula she was free to go, but not to leave the area as she would want to talk to her again. Jackie said she wanted a word with me before I left, so the constable took Paula back to reception to wait.

"Well!" Jackie said as she whistled out a breath

"Danny's already cheated on her several times. Behind closed doors, the marriage is toxic. Paula's had a rough time with him. Why are you so sure it was Carlton?"

"Overwhelming evidence, Madison. There are things you don't know. When I spoke to Carlton originally, he said he hadn't been on Harper's boat, but we found his fingerprints, and traces of his DNA. His knuckles were damaged, bruised, and Harper was beaten before he was killed. After we arrested Carlton, forensics examined his phone. He'd received a series of nasty texts from Harper—and I mean nasty. The first ones expose Carlton's affair with Paula, and Harper threatened to tell Danny. Later ones ridicule Paula for being pregnant, intimating that the baby wasn't Danny's or Carlton's, and the final few claimed the baby was his—Harper's. He said he had had sex with her—except he put it far more crudely, with graphic descriptions. Now Paula's corroborated what Carlton told us about his movements earlier that night. After he left Paula, he says he went to have it out with Harper, but he wasn't home, so he went back to his own boat."

[93]

I said, "He went on Harper's boat? Why the hell didn't he say so to start with?"

Jackie shrugged. "Fear? Panic? It didn't look good. He said he got on the stern. The door was open. He went in, looked around, came out—that's all. He said he bruised his knuckles fixing his car. But there's one more thing, and it's a clincher. The knife used to kill Harper was from the B&B kitchen, and guess what?"

"It had Carlton's fingerprints on it. Oh, Lord!" Jackie was right, it did seem open and shut.

"Anyway, that's not what I wanted to speak to you about."

"Oh?"

"I'm pissed off with Jill and Adam. I spoke to Jill, and my gov'nor spoke to Adam. Neither of them thought to mention they owned Harper's boat. I found that out today when backgrounds came back on them."

"It doesn't matter now, does it?" I said.

"See what you can find out. And you can tell Paula about Carlton's phone messages."

"Why didn't you?"

"Better it comes from you. Make her think you're confiding in her. See what else she says."

"I don't like this—besides, she didn't tell me about Sonia, so I'm not much of a confidante."

Jackie shrugged. "And let me know anything interesting Jill and Adam tell you."

I frowned.

"What if I don't want to?"

"That's fine. I'll interview them anyway, and you won't know what's been said," she grinned.

I wasn't happy with this arrangement, but on the other hand, I wanted to know what they were going to say. I'd discovered Harper's body on the boat I was living in, so I felt I was a valid stakeholder, and entitled to know—at least that was my excuse.

"Why didn't he say something to me?" Paula wailed as she drove us home. "He never even hinted that he thought I was pregnant. "What the hell have I done Madison?"

"The right thing. Whatever happened, you had to tell the truth." I tried a positive spin. "The DS said all you've done is confirm Carlton's movements and told them you're not pregnant."

"I still don't know why Harper and Carlton thought I was. I only told Danny, so unless he said something—"

I told her about the texts.

"Oh hell. Danny must have told Harper—that's the only explanation. I wish I'd never lied to Danny." She sank back in her seat. "But why would Danny tell Harper? And why did Harper add his own lies in the texts? In fact, why did Harper text Carlton at all?"

Why indeed, I thought.

"Don't say anything to Danny, Paula. Not a word," I said.

She assured me that he was the last person she wanted to speak to, or even see.

When we arrived back at Barrow View, I told Paula I was going up to my room to pack my things. Paula offered to help me get them to the boat, but I hadn't brought much up to the house, and I said I'd be fine.

"Listen," she said, "I'm sorry about earlier—up at the barrow. I thought Danny had put you up to snooping on me. There was a moment when I wondered if you were one of his women—I wouldn't put it past him, but I should've thought better of you. I'm sorry."

"Don't worry about it," I hugged her.

"I don't know what to think about Carlton," she said. "I thought I knew him. I don't want to believe it, but I'm so afraid that he may have killed Harper."

"I wish I could say something to help." We hugged again, and I went upstairs.

Chapter 14

I was back on Mercury at last. I'd moved the police tape which surrounded the boat. I looked at the bloodstain in the well-deck and shuddered. There wasn't much, and it should clean up easily, but still, it was a poignant reminder that this was not a dream—or rather a nightmare.

I put the kettle on for a cuppa. I wanted to sit down so much, but I couldn't forget the well-deck. It was preying on my mind, and I would never get any peace until it was cleaned up. It was grim work but didn't take long. I was clearing away the hose I'd used to wash everything down when there was a voice behind me.

"Hello, lass." It was Freda.

"Freda! Am I pleased to see you." I was in a strange mood—I wanted to be on my own, but I also wanted company.

"Can Jill join us too?"

"Of course. The more, the merrier."

"And I've brought the wee cat home too," she said as she set Ember down. Ember stood and looked around, then began to wind herself around my legs, purring and rubbing up against me.

The girls had come over to find out what was going on. They had both watched Carlton's arrest a few hours earlier. Jill had been shocked and had gone to find to Freda. When they saw me arrive back, they decided to find out what I knew. I couldn't believe my luck, as Jill was the very person I needed to talk to, but I wasn't sure how much she would say in front of Freda.

I washed my hands, feeling a bit like Lady Macbeth, put the kettle on again, and found more cups. I was able to share why Carlton had been arrested in general terms, but I couldn't tell them everything, and thankfully they didn't expect me to know.

As I was talking, I couldn't help noticing that although Freda was asking questions, Jill said nothing and looked out of sorts. I decided not to challenge her in front of Freda. The conversation drifted onto other topics. As we talked, I sorted out Ember's food and litter tray and then sat on the floor, fussing her as she ate. She began winding herself round my legs again. I tidied up and mentioned that I would need to do some shopping soon. Freda said she would run me to the shops tomorrow if I liked.

Time was getting on. "Forget tea," I said, and I opened a bottle of wine. I would have to catch Jill some other time. There were some admirable attempts at small-talk, but eventually, the topic drifted back to where it had begun, with the arrest of Carlton.

"It's a terrible thing," Freda said as she drained her glass. She looked as if she was about ready to leave. "So if Harper was killed around two, Carlton would have been coming back down to the moorings the same time. I must have missed him."

"What do you mean?" I asked.

"I never saw him."

"You were up at two?"

"Aye. Well, I don't know exactly what time it was, but I wake up around two regular as clockwork to visit the smallest room. On the way back, I peered around the curtain to see what the weather was doing. I saw Adam, but not Carlton."

We both looked at Jill.

"You saw Adam?" she asked. Was it my imagination, or was there a flash of panic in Jill's face?

"Aye," Freda explained, "he was up by the gate. If Carlton killed Harper, maybe Adam saw him?"

"Did you tell the police?" I asked.

"Of course," Freda laughed. "but I didn't think anything of it. I know he gets home late at night."

"What else happened?"

"I don't know. I went back to bed."

Jill must have noticed my quizzical expression.

"I told the police Adam was late too," she said. Whatever had unnerved her, she had already re-established her composure. "He works at Manny's, Madison, a club in town. He's often late back. He works the evenings in the bar, until eleven, but because of the barbecue he went in late and worked a late shift, from ten until closing. By the time he's helped clear up, he usually gets back around three. It was quiet Thursday morning, and they let him off early."

"Right," I said slowly, trying to process what she was saying. Was I the only one who wasn't up and about in the small hours of that morning? "Did he come straight back?"

"Yes, he was home by half one."

"How did he get those bruises then?" asked Freda.

If Jill was perturbed by the question, she hid it well. I looked back at Freda in admiration. She didn't miss much.

[99]

"What bruises?" I asked.

"I happened to notice the other day. On his left arm." She put her right hand a little below her left shoulder and looked at Jill, her expression as innocent as the day is long.

"There was a fight at the club. It happens sometimes," Jill said quickly. "Did the police mention Adam at all?"

"No," I lied. Then I had a thought, "except that they know you two own Harper's boat."

"Oh, what? They didn't already know?"

I shook my head.

"They spoke to us separately. The woman spoke to me. She never asked, and I never thought to say. Someone else spoke to Adam. I suppose he didn't tell them either. It wasn't deliberate. There's no big secret."

An awkward hush fell, which Jill eventually filled. "We bought it for Adam's sister, Sonia. It's so tragic Madison. She went off the rails as a teenager, and it's been a downhill spiral. She got in with the wrong crowd at school, started drinking and taking drugs. She was Adam's baby sister, and he felt responsible for her. He tried so many times to help her. He took her to AA meetings, paid for drug rehab, but nothing worked. Long story short, she ended up more than a junkie."

"Oh, no! How so?" I asked.

"Two or three months ago, she was arrested carrying drugs through an airport in the far east. There's no messing about over there. It's life in prison."

"I'm so sorry, Jill."

"I can't say I knew her particularly well, but her lifestyle was tearing Adam apart. A few months before her arrest, she phoned him. He said she sounded positive. The best he'd heard her in years. She told him she wanted to have a serious try at giving up. They talked about options. Adam offered for her to stay with us, but she wanted her own space, so he told her he would buy her her own boat. Somewhere she could call home. She could stay there while they decided what to do. She liked the idea. He said she sounded excited, and asked him to go ahead. She said she'd come back to England as soon as she could. The mooring at the far end of Ducks in a Row had recently come up, so Adam grabbed it and bought Red Rum for her. It's been a strain on our finances, but we've managed. Then we heard nothing for a while. Her phone number went dead, which was par for the course. Each number she rang from generally only lasted a few weeks. Then we heard that she'd been arrested for smuggling and was on remand in prison awaiting a court date. Soon after that Adam got a text from her on another burner phone, she must've got hold of it in prison. She said that she had a boyfriend, Harper, and she'd told him to go to the boat and wait for her to join him. She said if he turned up, she wanted Adam to help him. She was convinced she wouldn't be convicted— she hinted she was going to do a deal with the authorities and would make it home. Then we heard she'd committed suicide."

"No!"

"That was the official story, but another British inmate who knew Sonia smuggled a letter out to their family. She said Sonia was killed by the drugs gang she'd been working for."

"She'd been smuggling for them?" I was shocked.

"Apparently."

Jill finished her wine and stared at the glass. I gave her some more—it was the least I could do.

"The drugs gang probably realised what she was up to—that she was going to talk."

"Poor wee lass."

"That's terrible. Then Harper turned up?"

"No. He'd already arrived—we hadn't heard that Sonia had died at that point. At first, Adam welcomed him, but it quickly became apparent that Harper was a nasty piece of work. He drank and was obviously on drugs. After we found out about Sonia, all we wanted was for him to go—as soon as possible."

"Not with the boat?" I suggested.

"No. Adam had already disabled it."

"It was good of you to help him as much as you did," said Freda.

"Well, I guess if Sonia loved him, it was the least we could do. But Adam told him he couldn't stay forever, that we were planning on selling the boat."

"How did Harper take that?" I asked.

"He whinged a bit, but knew he couldn't stay."

It was all desperately sad, I thought, but somehow Harper didn't seem the sort of person to 'whinge'. It seemed to me that there was more to this than Jill was saying.

Chapter 15

After Jill and Freda left, I made myself something to eat. Ember and I watched some TV and I went to bed.

I had a lot to think about, but I was exhausted and fell asleep as soon as my head hit the pillow.

Something must have woken me in the night. I turned over and tried to get back to sleep, but realised I needed the bathroom. I sighed and got out of bed. On the way back, I paused and looked out of the window. With no moon, everything was in shades of indigo and black, shrouded in darkness. I could make out the darker outline of the house and tried to imagine the scene Freda had seen, with Adam up at the gate by the house. I laughed to myself—her eyesight must be bloody good. If someone was standing up by the gate now, I might be able to make out a shadow, but I definitely wouldn't know who it was. Maybe the moon was out or something. I yawned and headed back to bed.

The following morning I woke and made breakfast. The weather was cool but dry. I had some shopping to do, and although Freda had offered me a lift into town, I wanted some 'me time'.

It had been a traumatic few days. How ever much we wanted to believe otherwise, it did seem that Carlton was guilty. The best we could hope for was that there was a fight and it was self-defence. I felt so sorry for Paula. No sooner had she found someone who made her happy than he was taken away. I'd liked Carlton too, and he was a fantastic chef, but who knows what people are thinking, and what they are capable of.

I needed to move on. I had my own life to think about.

After putting it off over the past couple of days, I finally plucked up courage, set up my laptop and Skyped Isla. After she'd freaked out, she realised that I was fine and in no danger. She didn't seem surprised about Harper's death but was stunned at the news that Carlton had killed him.

"It's hard to take in Madison. I liked Carlton, and he was one hell of a chef."

"I know. That's exactly what I was thinking."

"I always felt it was only a question of time before someone got to Harper, but I thought it would be one of his 'business associates'."

"So, you knew him?" I asked. For some reason, it hadn't occurred to me that Isla had met Harper.

"Yes, he turned up, I don't know, six weeks or so before I left."

"To say 'hi' in passing?"

"More than that. He was Sonia's boyfriend, so he was bound to be a jerk, but I made an effort to make him feel welcome, for her."

"So you knew Sonia too."

"Yeah, about a year ago she came to stay with Adam for a while, and we hung out a bit. She was in a bit of state, but we got on well, and I liked her. Then she was gone. If she could get clean, I reckon we could've been good mates—but I don't do drugs."

"You knew the boat Adam bought was for her?"

"Yes, and I was looking forward to seeing her again. I guess I thought I might be able to help. Then Harper turned up."

"Did he try it on with you? He did with me."

She laughed.

"Madison, it's me you're talking to! Sonia had told me about him, so I had him bang to rights before we met. He had no chance to try anything with me. I laid down the law. He behaved. He was a better looker than I expected, though. I could understand what Sonia saw in him in that department—nice bit of eye candy." I smiled to myself. Freda must have got the phrase from Isla. "Then Adam told me about Sonia's death."

I thought for a moment.

"How did Harper take it?"

"Stoically. I don't know. Next time I saw him, I told him how sorry I was. He was quiet and seemed upset, but not distraught. I waited for him to talk about it, but he never did. Then I was busy with planning and packing—and Steve came over to stay for the last couple of weeks. I still saw harper, and when I did try to pry, he shrugged it off, and I didn't persist."

"One more thing—how did Harper get on with Carlton?"

"Neither of them ever mentioned the other to me. As far as I was aware, they were on nodding terms."

"So why would Harper care about Carlton and Paula?" I mumbled, half to myself.

"Carlton and Paula?" Isla had heard my muttering. "He never knew about them."

"You knew?"

"Seriously? I know everything!" she laughed.

I should have spoken to her earlier. "And Harper knew too."

"Harper? No, that's impossible, Madison!" She was adamant. "He didn't get it from me, and I'm pretty certain I was the only one who knew. I can talk for England, but I'm not a gossip. He barely knew anything about the others. He wasn't interested in any of them, and he certainly didn't know about Paula and Carlton."

"But he sent Carlton texts—"

"Texts!" she laughed again.

"Why? What's funny?"

"He was a tech philistine."

"But he had a phone, right?"

"Yeah, he had a phone. Not a smartphone—one of those cheap sim-only things."

"Like a burner phone?"

"I guess. But he rarely had any credit on it. Occasionally he would receive a call or text—probably drugs-related. If he ever needed to send a text or make a call, he'd put a couple of quid of credit on it down at the post office, and a couple of times when he ran out, he borrowed mine."

"Yours?"

"Yes, once for a call and a couple of times for texts. I insisted on listening in and vetting the texts. He wasn't going to use me for his pushing! It was all about meeting up with mates—although they probably weren't mates—although it sounded innocent enough."

"Where did he keep his phone?"

"The few times I went on his boat, it was lying around, on the side or on a table. He never kept it on him, and he only switched it on to use it."

"You should tell the police this."

"Should I? Give them my number, then. Oh, yes— I'm off on a trip inland, and the signal will be terrible. They may have trouble contacting me."

We changed the subject, and for a while, she told me all about Australia. Then I gave her a tour of the boat to show her that it was all good. She called out to a totally bemused Ember, who recognised her voice but insisted on looking everywhere except at the laptop screen, which we both found hysterical. I told her I was thinking of taking Mercury out for a run. She thought it was a great idea.

"I'm so sorry about all this hassle, Madison. You're supposed to be on a chill-out getaway. Take the boat off. A week or so on the cut would give you some proper peace and quiet. It's a great time to be out—weather's getting better but the canals aren't busy yet."

"I think I might. It's lovely here, but I could do with some space."

I ended the call, thanking her again for letting me stay—and I meant it, in spite of everything that had happened. I wouldn't want to be anywhere else.

Chapter 16

I made coffee and thought about the trip. It would kill two birds: I couldn't be hassled by my neighbours or the police, and I would get away from the depressing talk in the aftermath of the murder.

I took a look at the map.

Hmm. If I followed the canal the way the boat was facing, an hour away there was a lock, then another soon after, and then the canal went through a village. I looked it up on my phone and checked whether it had a shop. It did. I could take a trip up that way, and get the shopping I needed, then I could moor up there for a bit, or make it a more extended cruise like Isla suggested.

Ember jumped up next to me and purred as she too looked at the map.

"What do you think, Ember? Fancy a little trip?"

I'm sure she did.

The more I thought about it, the more the plan appealed.

"Let's do it!" I said to Ember.

No time like the present, so I got on with pre-cruise checks. I made sure the weed-hatch was secure, checked the alternator belt tension, and topped up the engine oil and water. I checked the fuel level too, but it took me a few minutes to find the fuel gauge. I say 'fuel gauge', but in common with many canal boats, it was no more than a stick to dip into the fuel tank, with a mark on it to indicate full and half-full levels. There was plenty. Isla had told me in her instructions that Ember would be delighted to go cruising, she loved it, but I was to make sure she couldn't get out while the boat was moving. I closed the doors and windows and pulled the curtains so it wouldn't get too hot for her.

One of the disadvantages of cruising on a boat solo was that I'd need to be at the tiller all the time. No loo breaks or making tea until I moored up. The boat might only travel at around three miles an hour, but if I took my hand off the tiller, or lost concentration for a few seconds, she'd be liable to hit something. I put a few necessities close at hand near the tiller—a canal map, a bottle of water, a hat, some sunnies, some tissues, and some naughty snacks. Finally, I unplugged the mains electric cable and stowed it away.

The ignition key was hanging inside the stern door. I took a deep breath, put it in the ignition and turned it to the first position. The familiar high pitched beep began. I turned the key further, paused to allowed the plugs to warm—then a little tweak. The thirty-eight horse-powered diesel engine coughed obligingly into life and settled into its monotonous thumping tune.

Leaving the boat ticking over, I stepped off the stern and went to tell Freda that I was off. She'd already heard the engine and seemed surprised, and a little disappointed, that I wouldn't be around to gossip with.

I cast off the line at the bow, then the centre line. After checking there was no traffic coming along on the water, I walked to the front and pushed the bow gently from the bank so I could negotiate around Harper's boat. I went back to the stern, untied the final line, got back on. I pushed the lever into forward. This was the moment of truth. I'd not driven this boat before. It was

[109]

only fifty-foot long, and I'd driven plenty which were longer, but it wasn't any old narrowboat, it was my friend's home. The engine hum increased, and the boat glided gently towards the middle of the canal.

I was off, and I was excited.

It was a typical spring day. The hot spell of the past week or so had broken, and the sky looked overcast, threatening rain. I'd pulled on my mac at the last minute—so much for the improving weather that Isla expected. Having said that, it was extraordinarily lovely. Trees along one side, and cows the other. They nonchalantly watched me pass as they ruminated. I think the NHS should prescribe off-season narrowboating to combat stress.

After around an hour, I reached the first lock. There was no-one around, and I'd not met another boat yet. I moored up at the lock landing and nipped into the boat to put the kettle on and check on Ember. I found a windlass, which I needed to open the lock paddles, and went up to set the lock. I was heading uphill, and the lock was half full of water, so I needed to empty it first. I opened the paddles and sat on one of the gate arms while the water level slowly dropped.

As I sat there, my mind drifted back to Ducks in a Row.

According to Jill, Adam had come straight back from the club and was home by half-one. Freda saw him up by the gate. She wasn't sure of the time, possibly around two. On reflection, she hadn't said he was heading to his boat. Had she almost implied he was waiting there? If so, what was he waiting for?

The lock had emptied sufficiently. I pushed open the gate on my side and cranked down the gate paddle to close it. Then I walked up to the top set of gates, crossed to the other side of the canal, opened the gate on the opposite side, and dropped that gate paddle too. It took longer, but I wasn't going to risk the paintwork by squeezing Mercury through one gate. I made my way back round to the boat, went inside and finished making my cup of tea. Then I started Mercury up, pulled off the lock landing and manoeuvred her into the lock. Once she was in, I clambered onto the roof of the boat, grabbed the centre line and climbed out of the lock using the lock ladder. I was glad there were no gongoozlers watching as it was not the most graceful lock I'd ever worked. My leg twinged a bit, which made all the scrambling around awkward—but a couple of weeks ago, I would have struggled a lot more. I looped the centre line around a bollard, closed the lower gates and then carefully opened the paddles at the top end to fill the lock. As the water rose, I stood on the side, holding the centre line to keep Mercury steady.

As I watched the lock fill, I thought about Carlton's activity that fateful night. He had spent half the night with Paula and got up a little before two to go back to his boat. Presumably, that was his habit—they were still trying to keep their affair a secret.

Carlton must have crept out of the house and made his way down to Ducks in a Row. He had definitely gone to visit Harper, he had admitted as much to Jackie—but why? What was he planning to do? Simply pull out a knife and kill him? If he did, he must have gone to the kitchen first to get the knife, and he must have had in mind what he was going to do, which meant it couldn't have been done in the heat of the moment. Unfortunately, it also meant that it wasn't a fight that got out of hand. He would never have planned a clumsy murder that was bound to lead back to him. It didn't sound like Carlton. He said he got on the boat and walked through it, but Harper wasn't there. Maybe Carlton went off looking for him and found him outside somewhere.

"Hello!" said a voice. It made me jump.

"Oh, hi."

A woman had appeared. She was holding a windlass. I looked up the canal. There was a boat slowly edging towards the lock.

"We're heading down. I'll finish this lock if you like."

"Oh, are you sure?" I glanced at the water level. The lock had filled up while I'd been daydreaming.

"Of course," she said. "I'll do the other gate if you can do this one?"

It's lovely when you come across another boat with a crew, and they recognise how awkward it can be cruising single-handed. Once she'd crossed over the gates to the other side, I opened my side, wound down the paddle and got back on the boat. Now the lock was full it was simple to step onboard, so no embarrassing blundering around. While the woman opened the gate on her side and lowered the paddle, I started up the engine and took the boat out of the lock, thanking her as I passed.

The morning continued, delightfully uneventful. An hour later, I went through the next lock, which was quicker and easier as it was already empty. After a further half-hour cruising, I reached the outskirts of the village, and I found a spot to moor up. I was feeling hungry, so I made myself a wrap, and put the kettle on for a cup of tea. I let Ember out and ate my wrap on the towpath, watching

[112]

her. She sat in the middle of the path and looked around. Oh, we've moved, she seemed to say, let's see what's here. I'd heard of ships' cats, and I knew cats were not uncommon on narrowboats, but I was still tickled to see how unfazed Ember was by her change of scenery. She seemed totally indifferent to the new location. She sauntered across to the hedge. After five minutes of exploring, it began spitting with rain. She ambled back to the boat, and both of us got back on board.

After lunch, I grabbed my mac and backpack, locked up the boat and headed out to the village.

The rain wasn't too bad, more a drizzle. In spite of that, it was a lovely walk, and my leg was holding up far better than I'd expected. There was only a dull ache, which was amazing considering I'd spent the morning standing up, I'd been through two locks, and now I was walking to the village.

As I walked, my mind started drifting again. If Adam had left the club around one in the morning, and if he came straight back, he would have been back at Ducks in a Row by about quarter to two at the latest. That was around the time Paula said Carlton left her. I wondered whether they'd seen each other. Surely Carlton would have told Jackie if he'd seen Adam, and Adam would have told Jill if he'd seen Carlton. They can't have missed each other by much.

Then there were the strange injuries. Did Carlton hurt his hand fixing his car? Did Adam get the bruise on his arm in a fight at the club? What if they had met up, and had some sort of argument. Perhaps they'd had a fight, and maybe that was what Jill was cagey about—but what did they have to fight about?

After twenty minutes, I'd reached the shop.

"Hello," I said to the man behind the counter.

"Hi," he replied, smiling as he looked up from his paper.

I grabbed a basket and wandered around, finding the things I needed. I spotted a couple of things Freda might like, so I grabbed those too. The man cleared his paper away and began scanning my items as I stacked them up.

"Passing through?" he asked.

"Yes, I'm moored down on the canal."

"Many boats there?"

"No. I'm the only one."

He snorted, "A few weeks ago—over the Easter holiday, it was boats from one end to the other."

"It's a lot easier to get through the locks now."

"True," he admitted. "That's twelve-twenty, please."

I tapped my card on the machine.

"Receipt?" he asked.

"No, thanks."

"You staying long?"

"No, heading further up," I said as I unslung my backpack, and started putting my purchases in.

"A lot of people move on when they realise the phone signal here isn't great."

He wasn't the greatest advocate for the village, but I played along.

"Funny you should mention that. Do you know what? I've not even thought about my phone since I set out. I always carry it with me," I patted my pocket, "but I don't use it much, it's more a habit."

"That's the way to live. We should throw the damn things away." He pointed to an article in the paper he'd been reading. "See that? The bastards can hack into your phone and send you messages that look like they come from your bank, or credit card company or whatever."

"Yeah," I said. "Sometimes I think it'll get to the point where we can't use them anymore."

I slung my pack onto my back. We said goodbye, and I headed back to the boat.

Talking of phones, I wondered, what happened to Harper's? Isla said he had a burner which he hardly used, and Jackie talked about the texts Carlton had received from Harper, but she never mentioned the phone itself, and I never asked. Surely the police must have found it, and looked up Harper's phone records from his provider?

Still, I thought, it's nothing to do with me now.

Thinking about phones reminded me that I hadn't passed Isla's number on to the police yet. If I didn't do it soon, they might not be able to get hold of her. I guessed I'd have to use my phone after all. I checked it, and as the man in the shop had told me, the signal wasn't great, but I had one bar. I phoned Jackie, gave her Isla's number and told her about our Skype conversation.

"Well, that's interesting," she said when I was done talking. "I'll make a note of the number." She didn't sound enthusiastic.

"Are you going to ring her?"

"Yes, Madison, thank you for passing this on to me, but it's always difficult—taking a statement from people who are abroad. I can talk to her, but I can't use anything she says as part of the case unless she goes to a local police station and makes a formal statement. It sounds as if that's not going to happen."

"Hmm. Did you get much from Harper's phone?"

"Nothing—it was never found."

"Oh!" I thought for a moment. "Isla said he definitely had a phone."

"As she said, it was probably a burner, and we can't trace it."

"Hmm. I suppose that's the whole point about burners."

"Exactly. We've no trace of it, or of the number he used. The texts Carlton received were from an unknown number. Harper covered his tracks well. He was an experienced drug-pusher. He lived in a world where manipulation and blackmail were commonplace—from the enquires I've made into his past, he was an expert at it."

"I don't understand. You're saying Harper sent texts to Carlton, and made an effort to cover his tracks—but he told Carlton his name?"

"That's how these people work. In the drugs world, you want people to know who's threatening you, but you don't want any official trace back to you. Oh, and Harper's not his real name either."

"I'm not surprised about that. One other thing, Isla said he was useless at tech."

"It's more likely that he's expert at making people think that— his life depended on it. The bottom line, Madison, is that however he did it, he found out about Carlton and Paula, and he found out that Paula told Danny she was pregnant. He used that information to send out feelers to see who could be blackmailed—it's a classic play. Don't underestimate Harper—he was a professional con man."

"I guess."

"And he picked the wrong person with Carlton, who went over to confront him, and—whatever happened between them—Carlton lost it."

"Hmm. Maybe." I still wasn't convinced. I was almost back at the boat. "But you will ring Isla?" I asked.

"Of course I will, and if she says anything that might help, or affect the case, I'll see if I can arrange for her to make a statement."

"Okay, thanks, Jackie."

"No, thank you—any help anyone can offer is always welcome. Now get on with your trip, and try to forget all of this."

"Okay, I will—oh, one last question. When did Carlton receive the first text from Harper?"

After we ended the call, I checked the calendar on my phone. Isla was adamant that Harper had no interest in Carlton, but Jackie was convinced he was an expert in deception. He'd certainly pulled the wool over Isla's eyes, because, looking at the dates, he must have known about Paula ten days before Isla left for Australia.

I got back to the boat and packed away my shopping. The rain had stopped, and it was brightening up. I was tempted to stay put, exactly where I was. It was a lovely spot. In the end, and after consulting Ember, who was indifferent, I decided to do a couple more hours' cruising. I cast off and headed on up the canal. If I did two more hours today, tomorrow I should be able to get up past Norton Junction and onto the Leicester line. Perhaps I could spend a few days moored around Crick.

I stood at the tiller and tried to focus on the beautiful countryside that I was passing. Spring was beginning to take hold, and the birds in the woods off to one side of the canal were singing away for all they were worth. Much to my annoyance, however, I couldn't help mulling over Carlton's texts and Harper's phone. Why did Harper care about Paula and Carlton? If he was sending texts from a burner, what was he trying to achieve—it's not as if there was a drugs deal at stake, or maybe there was? But Carlton hated anything to do with drugs.

A duck began quacking madly, and suddenly three of them took off noisily, heading down the canal, wrapped up in romantic squabbles of their own.

I mulled over Isla's comments again—that Harper hadn't known about Paula and Carlton. Surely he must have found out and not told her. Jackie must be right, and Isla wrong—in which case, what was Harper's motive for provoking Carlton? Blackmail, like Jackie had suggested? Or something else?

A gentle breeze whispered through the trees and rippled over the still water ahead. Then I spotted a winding hole up ahead, where the canal widened to allow boats to turn around. It seemed prophetic.

"Oh, damn!" I yelled to a pair of swans who were serenely gliding along, they looked up at me, puzzled, as they gently slid past.

I wanted to carry on cruising and enjoy my time away, but I couldn't help myself.

I turned around in the winding hole, and I was soon heading back towards Ducks in a Row.

Jackie said the mystery surrounding the texts was not significant, but it was—it was hugely, massively significant.

If only I knew why.

Chapter 17

It was evening by the time I reached Ducks in a Row.

All the way back, I'd been having doubts about what I was doing. A man had been arrested, and if there was sufficient evidence, he would be charged, then it would be up to a jury. It was nothing to do with me. That was all well and good, but the more I thought about it, the more things didn't add up.

The following morning, I got up, had breakfast, and pottered around the boat. Ember had accepted our return to the moorings with all her usual feline grace and indifference. When I let her out, there was a brief moment of confusion as she adjusted to the fact that the boat was back in the same place, but facing the other way. She quickly papered over the embarrassment of her disorientation and sauntered off to re-visit old haunts.

Later in the morning, I called in on Freda.

"Hi!" I responded to her enthusiastic call to come in. I ducked into her boat.

"Hello, lass. Ye had a good trip out?"

"Yes, I did thanks. I picked up a couple of things for you," I said, as I handed her a tub of her favourite hot chocolate and the latest issue of the gossip magazine she liked.

"Oh, thank you," she smiled broadly, which warmed my heart.

As she went to put the kettle on, I made her stop for a moment so I could look at her properly.

"Hey, I love your hair. Really—I'm not just saying that. Was it Rose?"

"Aye," she looked bashful. "I decided to take the plunge."

"She's done an amazing job."

"She's a canny lass. I think she's going to be doing everyone around here now. Both Veronica and Alice are in the queue, but I think it's Jill next, later today."

"Hello?" said a timid voice.

"Oh, speak of the devil," grinned Freda. "Come on in my dear. We were all talking about our style guru."

Rose came in and smiled nervously.

I complimented her on what a wonderful job she had done on Freda's hair and joked that it must have been a real challenge—at which Freda laughed and told Rose that it's easy to go off people.

Rose smiled at the banter but said nothing.

We settled down to our drinks, and although I tried to keep the conversation on hair, fashion, canals, boats—anything—it eventually turned to the inevitable subject. We agreed that it was immensely upsetting.

I'd noticed that the tape surrounding Harper's boat had gone. Freda said the previous day the police had turned up, taken the tape away, and told Jill and Adam that they were free to go on the boat.

Yet again, we went over the movement of various people on the night in question. With Carlton not speaking to the police, it was difficult to come to any conclusion other than that he was

[121]

guilty. He must have killed Harper. What we still couldn't grasp, was what Harper's motives were in sending the texts, and why Carlton reacted the way he did. The only explanation was that he lost control and things got out of hand, which didn't tally with him taking along a knife.

Rose softly spoke up, "Well, I still think Harper was lush."

"Cotton candy," Freda said.

"Eye candy," I corrected her with a smile.

"Aye, that's the one."

We pointed out some of Harper's failings to Rose, as gently as we could.

"Oh, I didn't want to go out with him. He may have looked nice," she continued, "but he was horrible to Sonia."

"Oh, was he?" I asked.

"Mmm, I heard Jill and Adam talking." She looked embarrassed. "I didn't mean to eavesdrop, but our boat's nose to nose with theirs and if both bow doors are open, I can't help but overhear."

We fell silent, wondering what Rose had overheard, but not wanting to push her.

Then she spoke again.

"It was his fault," she said.

Freda and I looked at her, puzzled.

"Sonia being caught."

"How did they know that?" I asked.

"Harper told Adam when he was drunk." Then she added for

[122]

clarity, "Harper was drunk, not Adam."

"Oh!"

Jill hadn't mentioned this when we'd spoken—only that he was a nasty piece of work and they'd wanted him gone.

Rose had more to say.

"Adam said Harper was using Sonia to smuggle drugs back from the far east. When they got to the airport, Harper knew straight away something was up."

"He was using Sonia as a drugs mole?" said Freda incredulously.

"Mule," I said, stifling a grin.

Rose nodded, "Yes, that's the word they used, mule. It was horrible. She had to swallow packets of drugs to get them through customs. When Harper realised the police were onto them, he hit her in the stomach to try to rupture the bags, so she would get ill, and he could make off in the confusion. It didn't exactly work, but he managed to get away all the same."

"Oh my Lord, the poor wee lass!" Freda exclaimed with her hand to her mouth.

"Poor lass indeed," I echoed. "I knew Harper was bad news— but that's shocking."

"Adam was distraught," Rose said. "He was raging about it."

"I'm not surprised."

Rose stopped talking and wriggled shyly, but we waited for more.

She got the message and carried on. "Adam said that when

[123]

Harper first turned up, he gave him the benefit of the doubt. But when Harper told him what had happened, boasted about it—how he had got away, Adam was seething. Then when he heard Sonia had died in prison, he blamed Harper—said it was his fault she was killed."

Freda and I were stunned at Rose's revelation. If Jackie had known all this, she had certainly kept it close to her chest.

The conversation died away. Rose soon left, and I headed back to my boat. This changed everything. Up to now, I'd had to agree that Carlton was the most likely killer. It made sense, with the evidence and his background, even if the motive was dubious. However, there was now someone else who had a more than adequate motive. He had also been out and about that night. Having said that, the timings didn't work out—Adam was back on his boat half an hour before Harper was killed—but was he? We only had Jill's word on that.

I sat with Ember on my knee. I closed my eyes and walked through everything I now knew: Carlton leaving Paula in the middle of the night, his hurt hand, his fingerprints on Harper's boat, the kitchen knife used for the killing, Adam's motive, Adam's injured arm, the time he arrived back from work, Danny telling Harper about the baby, and Harper's missing phone.

I stroked Ember, and she purred. I was going round and round in circles: Carlton and Paula, damaged hand, fingerprints, kitchen knife, Adam's arm, the timings, Harper's phone, Paula's baby, Carlton and Paula—round and round again and again.

It was like a jigsaw, muddled and confused. Tip it out of the box, it's a complete mess—a complete muddle, with pieces upside-down and back to front. I didn't even know what picture I was trying to make—I was still stumbling through the mist, trying to make out the shapes.

Turn the pieces the right way up, find the corners and the edges and begin there.

Turn the pieces.

Find the edges.

Move them around.

Oh!

I sat up startled, and Ember leapt off my lap, complaining bitterly.

I fired up my laptop. It took about an hour to confirm my suspicions and uncover the other pieces I had been missing.

Of course—there it was.

I now had all the pieces—most of them had been there all the time, but I'd been trying to make the wrong picture.

Ember was looking up at me.

"Do you know what this means?" I asked her.

Ember probably did. She seemed to know everything.

I needed to prove beyond doubt that I was looking at the right picture, and I knew how to do it.

I picked up my phone and called Freda—I needed a number, and then with shaking hands, I sent a text to Adam.

Chapter 18

I paused and looked back down the track through the trees.

There was no-one around.

I was pleased with how my leg was holding out. It was only a couple of days since I'd been up to the long barrow with Paula. Although it was aching, I was sure that it wasn't nearly as bad this time.

I looked at my phone.

No messages.

The meeting was fixed for seven. I wanted to make sure I arrived early. At this rate, I should be there by quarter to.

It was still light, but with the recent dull weather, the woods were particularly gloomy.

I took one more look behind me, but there was no-one in sight.

I zipped my mac up further. I wished I'd worn a thicker jumper now. Although I was in the woods, the wind was whipping through the trees and had a bitter edge. Once I was out in the open, it would be biting.

I paused as I emerged and admired the mound of the barrow. It was an incredible piece of engineering—all done by hand, thousands of years ago. I wondered how many people had stood in this exact spot and marvelled at it.

There was still no-one around, which was a good thing.

I went past the false doorway. As I rounded the mound, I was exposed to the full force of the wind. I was right—it was flipping freezing.

I made my way over to the bench and sat down, shivering as I waited.

It was not too long before I felt his presence. He was behind me, but I didn't look round. I continued to stare out over the valley, and the clouds scudding overhead.

He sat next to me.

"Hello, Adam," I said, "let's move inside. It's bloody cold out here."

I got up, and he followed.

I walked to the doorway and went in. Afterwards, I realised that I hadn't given a thought to the nesting swifts.

Inside it was dark, but I had a torch.

We stood in the main chamber. He had a torch too, and I waited while he fumbled around to recover it from one of the zipped up pockets in his coat.

"Let's move down to the end," I said.

The main chamber was large—much larger than it looked from outside. That was because as you entered, there was a slope down from ground level to floor-level inside. Like an iceberg, there was much more built into the hill than you could see from the outside. There were three chambers at the far end, behind where I was now standing.

"What do you think you know," he said.

"A lot more than you and Jill were prepared to tell the police," I said.

It was odd talking to a shadow. We both had our torches aimed at the ground, so all I could see was a vague dark shape. Outside the boundary of our lights, the chamber was pitch black. It was easy to imagine how in years gone by, any visitors, or even the original designers of the barrow, could have imagined ghosts in the shadowy gloom.

"I want to know what you're willing to pay first," I said.

"Whatever you think you know, you're wrong," he shook his head, I'd never had thought you were up for blackmail, Madison."

I shrugged. "So you're not a good judge of character."

"How do I know it's worth paying for?"

"Don't give me that." I raised my voice. The sound rose up to echo around the cavern but was instantly smothered by the oppressive darkness.

He stood silently.

"Don't even think about it," I said after a moment.

"What?"

"I told Freda I was meeting you."

"I might never have seen you. Or I might have found you dead!" He leaned in towards me and emphasised the word 'dead'. I took a step back.

"I've got texts from you," I countered.

He paused to think, and then said, "How do I know you'll keep your mouth shut?"

"I'll have to—it's no good me speaking up in three months time. I'll end up being done as an accessory."

There was silence.

"So?" he suddenly said, making me jump a little.

"You were seen, Adam. When you came back from work that night."

"And?"

"Freda saw you, around one forty-five." A calculated lie, I thought. "She didn't know the significance of it and didn't tell the police. She thought you were heading back to your boat."

"Wasn't I?"

"I saw you too." Another lie. "You where watching Carlton, weren't you? You spotted him as he made his way back from Paula. He went straight to Harper's boat. Harper had been winding him up about Paula, and he'd had enough. Carlton said that when he got to the boat, Harper wasn't there, but he was, wasn't he? Carlton beat him up, so when he left, he'd done half the job for you. All you had to do was waltz in and knife him."

"Why would I do that?"

"Harper was responsible for Sonia's death."

There was silence.

He moved away from me a few steps. I guessed he was thinking. Trying to decide his next move.

"You bitch," he said at last. "I ought to—"

"But you know you can't," I said. Then I added, "I think it's worth at least, hmm, thirty grand."

"Don't be stupid!" he yelled. "Where am I going to get that sort of money?"

"From the sale of Red Rum."

"Paula will notice."

"Not if you do it right. Say you sold her for less than you thought. Tell there was a problem with the survey, get a loan, I don't care, I'm sure you'll think of something."

"What if I said it wasn't me?"

"Won't wash. We both know it wasn't Carlton."

He laughed. "You've got it all wrong. You're barking up the wrong tree."

He swore at me a few more times and stormed off out the barrow.

I heaved a sigh of relief.

Now there was only the light of one torch, and the oppressiveness of the chamber had grown thicker and heavier.

I stayed put.

There was not a sound.

After a few more minutes, I was ready to give up when I heard a noise.

"Who's that?" I called.

"Hello, Madison," said an unseen voice. "Fancy meeting you here."

Chapter 19

I shone my torch up at him.

"Hi Danny," I tried to sound light—not sure I succeed. My heart was hammering. "What brings you here?"

He put his hand up to fend off the light, so I aimed my torch back down at the ground. I couldn't see whether he had a torch. If he had, it wasn't on.

"I come up here a lot," he said. "There's an atmosphere—an energy. It helps to clear my mind."

"I know what you mean. There is something about this place. Over the years, thousands of people must have stood here."

I wondered if any of them had the same questions in their mind that I had at that moment. Danny seemed hesitant. As if he was weighing up options. I could only guess at what those options might be.

After a long pause, he said, "It was about where you're standing now, that the two skeletons were found. Lying together in death, hand in hand."

The thought made me shudder, and I took a step back.

I wondered what their last thoughts might have been.

He seemed amused at my discomfort.

"More to the point," he continued, "what are you doing here?"

"Me? Like you—I think this is such an awe-inspiring place. I wanted to experience the atmosphere in the evening."

"I bet you did." He sounded menacing and took a step nearer. "So how is Adam?"

"Adam?" I asked as innocently as I could. I took another step back.

"Saw him leaving. Having a nice chat, were you? Or were you up to something else?"

"He's not my type."

"You were in here with him a while. Must have been something interesting."

"He was explaining about the excavations."

He laughed and took another step towards me. I took another step back, but I was getting close to the wall.

"You see," he said slowly, "and here's the thing. It wasn't excavations you were talking about."

"No?" I was trembling a little, and my leg had decided to ache.

"I heard what you said to Adam."

"Listening in, were you?"

"Trying to blackmail him, were you? Wanted to squeeze a few quid out of him, eh?"

"It all helps."

"So not the wide-eyed little innocent you make out to be."

"We all have to do what we can. So why are you really here? Following Adam?"

He didn't reply.

His hands were moving. I shone my torch on him—he was holding a knife.

I gasped, but I didn't cry out.

"You see, you've given me a little bit of a dilemma," he spoke calmly.

He stepped forward again. By now, I now had my back to the wall, but he was still ten feet away. I wanted to keep it that way.

He fumbled in another pocket and took out a torch. He did have one—that was a shame. I was hoping to be able to shine a light in his eyes to blind him if I needed to.

He flicked it on. It was way stronger than mine and lit up the whole chamber. Off to one side, about five feet along the wall I was backed up against, was one of the side chambers. It wasn't big, but it was something. I edged along towards it.

"Why have you got a knife, Danny?" I asked.

"To help me with my dilemma."

"Which is?"

"Don't move any further!" he shouted.

I jumped at his voice and froze.

"You see," he said as he stepped towards me, "I think you know more than you are saying. I don't think you're into blackmailing."

"Seemed a good plan. What's not to like?"

"You either know more than you're saying, or you'll soon work it out, and I can't risk that."

"Rubbish!" I yelled at the top of my voice.

"What?" he roared.

My yell had startled him for a second, but then he lunged toward me. I made a dash for the side chamber, but it was too far away. He grabbed me and pulled me towards him.

"Danny!" a voice called from behind him.

"What?" he roared again.

"Don't move!" The command rang out from a voice to my right. A shadow had emerged from the side chamber I had been heading towards.

I yelped as Danny grabbed me and held me in front of him. One arm gripped me tightly, the other was around my neck, holding the knife. He clumsily backed us both up into an awkward, low corner of the chamber.

I was shaking, with fear, or shock, or cold or all of them.

Two more shapes were making their way towards us along the main chamber.

"Get back!" Danny shouted.

"Don't be an idiot!" I recognised the voice. It was Jackie. "Do you want to add a second murder?"

"Shut up and stop moving, and you might not find out," he spat at her.

I could feel him breathing hard as he held me to him. This was not how he had planned things—come to think of it, this wasn't how I'd planned things either.

"You're going to get out of my way and let me past," Danny yelled. I could feel his panic.

[134]

My legs were like jelly. I didn't want to collapse. I wanted to cry out, but I dared not. The blade was pressed flat against my neck, directly on my wind-pipe.

"Then what?" Jackie asked calmly.

"I want to see Paula. I need to talk to her!"

I was shaking—uncontrollably. One twitch from Danny, and I would be taking my last breath. I tried to stay still. I tried to stop the trembling. I could hear voices speaking, but I didn't know what they were saying.

My head was reeling.

The world had become confused and distant.

Had he already cut my throat?

Was I dying?

Is this what it was like to die?

When I later recounted the events, I told everyone that I had passed out. Perhaps I had.

As I was held in his grip, with the cold blade against my throat, I saw two shapes appear in the darkness. I thought for a moment that it was Jackie and a policeman. Slowly the shadows of the chamber fell away, and an eerie twilight glow appeared all around me. I could see the whole chamber—the dirt floor, the stone walls and the ceiling. Danny had gone, so had Jackie and the others.

In front of me stood two people.

A man and a woman.

They were about my age and dressed in linen rags. They looked

[135]

dirty, and their hair was unkempt, but they both seemed curiously content. They looked at each other and smiled. The woman held out a hand. I reached out, and our fingertips touched. She took my hand in both of hers, and put something into my palm as she squeezed gently, reassuringly. I knew everything was going be to fine. I felt free, euphoric, and so happy that I wanted to sing and dance.

Then she let go.

Suddenly, I was back.

I felt calm.

I could hear voices, but they were muffled, and I didn't understand them.

Danny was holding me up with one arm. My head was slumped down, and my chin was resting on his hand.

He had moved the knife—it was pointing forward, threatening Jackie.

I knew what I had to do.

As I bit deeply into his hand. The last thing I heard was screaming.

They tried to get me to go to the hospital, but I refused.

I was on the bench outside the chamber surrounded by police and a couple of paramedics. They told me that when I had bitten Danny, he had dropped the knife and thrown me against the wall. They were concerned that I might have concussion as I had lost consciousness for a few seconds. I told them I was feeling fine. I mostly was fine—a bit woozy perhaps, but to be honest, all I wanted was to go back to the boat and have a glass of wine.

Two policemen helped me to Jackie's car, which was parked on an access track near the woods, so it wasn't far.

"I should never have agreed to this," she said as she steered the car down the bumpy track, "it was the stupidest of ideas."

"It worked fine," I insisted. "I couldn't shout out any earlier, he hadn't admitted enough. I had to get more out of him."

"You should have yelled 'Rubbish' as soon as he pulled the knife. I couldn't see clearly from where I was standing. You're a liability, you really are," she smiled, "but I'm glad you're okay."

She glanced over to see me staring at a small silver object in my hand.

"What's that?" she asked.

It was a beautifully made latticework of silver that might have been a pendant on a necklace or a charm on a bracelet. It looked ancient and reminded me of Celtic craftwork.

"I—er—found it," I said. I must have found it. I must have picked it up when I was thrown to the ground. "It's lovely, isn't it?"

"It's beautiful Madison."

Chapter 20

"Honestly lass, what a scrape you got into."

Freda was making me tea back on Mercury. I'd asked for wine, but she said tea would be better after a shock. I was laid out on the dinette sofa. Rose, Veronica, Alice and Jill were all crammed in, having rushed over to find out why the police were escorting me home.

Rose had been staring silently at the amulet.

"So it was all a setup?" she asked.

"It was," I replied.

"What made you suspect Danny in the first place?" asked Jill.

"Several things, including you two," I said, nodding to Jill and Freda.

"Us?" Freda looked at me, astonished.

"Yes. You, Jill, said on Saturday that Adam was home by half one on the night of the murder, but he wasn't, was he?"

Jill shifted nervously, but she didn't reply.

"It's okay, bear with me. The police already know he left work early—around twenty past one, and it takes half an hour to get back with no traffic, so he couldn't have been here before one-fifty. When Freda saw him up by the gate, it must have been a little before two. When you told me what you saw, Freda, you said he was up by the gate. Why didn't you say walking down from the gate, or on his way to this boat?"

"He may have been, lass."

"But that's not what you said. You said up 'by' the gate."

"Aye, well now you mention it, I only watched for a moment, but he didn't seem to be going anywhere. I never gave it a thought."

"Adam was back here around ten to two—you knew that, didn't you, Jill?"

"Madison," Jill looked panicked, "I don't want to hear—"

"Relax. I know what happened," I tried to look reassuring, but Jill wasn't buying it and got up to leave.

"Don't worry," I said. "Sit!"

She looked around at the others watching her—and resigned herself to sit down again.

"He got back as arranged at about one-fifty," I continued.

"As arranged?" Jill looked puzzled now.

"What you didn't know is that he had arranged a meeting with Carlton. After the barbecue, probably, they decided to teach Harper a lesson. I may as well tell you. It'll come out soon enough anyway. Carlton was having an affair with Paula. Paula didn't know that Danny had found out. Danny wanted to get back at Carlton but had no way of doing it. Danny had already tried to sack him, but Paula had vetoed it. Danny was too much of a coward to confront him, so any opportunity to punish Carlton was too good to miss."

"What opportunity?" asked Veronica.

"He found out Carlton and Adam were planning on teaching Harper a lesson."

"How did he find out?" asked Freda.

"I had a theory about that, but to be sure I had to carry out a little test—up at the long barrow. I texted Adam to meet me there—I'd briefed him first as to what I wanted him to do. And sure enough, Danny turned up too."

"But how did he know?"

I smiled.

"What was his job before he took over Barrow View?" I asked.

They talked amongst themselves and decided it was IT.

"Not just IT—that covers a multitude of sins," I said. "Paula told me he was in telecoms. When I looked him up, I found out he was a senior telecoms engineer working on mobile systems. And why did he leave?"

"To start the bed and breakfast with Paula?" volunteered Jill.

"No. He was forced to resign after a hacking incident. They suspected he was involved, but it was never proved."

"But how did he find out what Carlton and Adam were planning?"

"They must have phoned each other at some point, and he intercepted the call.

"Oh, he was hacking them," said Alice.

"He was. He'd been monitoring Paula's phone for some time—voice intercepts, reading texts and messages, that sort of thing. He started monitoring Carlton's after he found out Paula was having an affair with him."

"So on the night of the murder, he knew Carlton was going to meet up with Adam," said Freda.

"And why they were meeting, too. Oh, and Adam also knew about Carlton and Paula," I said. "Carlton had confided in him."

"What?" Jill looked shocked.

"He didn't tell you? They must be tight, those two. When Danny realised Carlton and Adam were best buddies, he began monitoring Adam too. He wanted to find out everything Paula was up to. That's why he picked up my text. He knew I was on to something, but even if I'd concluded it was Adam that killed Harper, he knew it was only a question of time before I realised my mistake. His method had worked once, so he thought it would work again. He planned on meeting me at the long barrow after I'd met Adam."

"His method?" asked Jill.

"I'll get to that. When the police examined Carlton's phone, they found more than enough motive to arrest him. A string of abusive messages from Harper, saying he knew about his affair with Paula, that he'd been having a relationship with her too, and that she was pregnant with his baby."

"Paula's pregnant? By Harper?" gasped Jill.

"No, she isn't. That's the point. Paula told Danny she was pregnant—to get back at him—but she refused to say whose it was. He believed her and guessed it was Carlton's. So Danny sent the texts to Carlton to provoke Carlton into thinking Harper had slept with Paula."

"Ah," suddenly Freda got it. "Danny was sending the texts, pretending to be Harper."

"Is that even possible?" asked Veronica.

"Texts are notoriously insecure, especially if you know what you're doing, and he did, having specialised in mobile phone tech. What he didn't know, was that Paula hadn't told Carlton, or anyone, that she was pregnant—"

"Because she wasn't," completed Jill.

I nodded.

"And the police agreed to you meeting up with Danny?" asked Jill.

"Not really. I told them what I was going to do. Jackie wasn't happy at all."

Freda had her thinking face on, and then asked, "Why was he bothering? Why didn't Danny set fire to Carlton's boat or something?"

"It would be too obvious. He wanted to hurt Paula as well as stitch Carlton up. I don't think he planned this, but it was too good an opportunity to miss. He could let Adam and Carlton do whatever they wanted to Harper, waltz in afterwards, and kill him. The worst scenario was that both Carlton and Adam would be arrested, but he was pretty confident he could pin it on Carlton alone."

"So neither of them hurt Harper, did they?" asked Veronica.

"I wouldn't say that. When Carlton left Paula, he met up with Adam—who was waiting by the gate. Freda, if you'd carried on watching Adam, you might have seen Carlton too. Then they went down to the boat to find Harper."

"Danny's plan was working," said Jill.

"It was working well. Maybe Harper got wind of what was going on, or maybe he saw Adam hanging about, but when they got down to Red Rum, he wasn't there. Carlton went on board to look for him. Then they searched the area and spotted him in the woods. They ran him down and beat him up. Enough to send him a message, but not enough to do major damage. Harper staggered back to his boat—"

"Followed by Danny, who had been watching," chipped in Jill.

"Exactly. He'd already lifted one of the knives which had Carlton's prints on from the kitchen. All he needed to do now was finish the job—and also make sure he threw his phone in the canal—because if the phone was checked, there would be no messages to Carlton. But Harper was tougher than he thought. He wasn't dead. He managed to crawl onto Mercury, seeking help, and that's where he died. It was a win-win for Danny. Carlton had been framed for murder, and if that didn't work, Adam was the next likely suspect. Not only did Adam have the opportunity—he got back earlier than both you and he admitted, Jill—he also had motive because of Sonia."

"Why didn't the police go after Adam?" Freda asked.

"They might have if the case against Carlton hadn't been so good."

Jill sighed. "I was so afraid that Adam had killed him, but he said Harper was fine when they left him. We decided Carlton must have gone back and killed him later."

We sat in silence, each lost in their own thoughts.

Then Rose spoke up. "What, erm—" She blushed as everyone looked at her.

"Go on," I said.

"Erm—what made you realise Harper didn't send the texts?"

"Good question," I said encouragingly. "It had always bothered me that his phone had disappeared. The police believe Carlton disposed of it."

"To hide the texts Harper had sent?" asked Freda.

"And yet he didn't try to hide his phone, or delete the texts he'd received."

"He didn't delete the texts? I would have," said Veronica.

"Maybe he wanted to confront Harper with them one day. Anyway, the point is why only dispose of part of the evidence? Perhaps there was something else compromising on Harper's phone, but I couldn't work out what. When Isla told me Harper was a tech dinosaur, it began to fall into place. Jackie told me Carlton had received the first fake text from Harper a few weeks before Isla left for Australia. Isla obviously didn't know about the texts, but she was sure Harper had no idea and no interest in who was sleeping with who. Then the penny dropped. The problem was that Harper's phone didn't have anything compromising on it."

"Because Harper didn't send the texts," said Jill, nodding gently.

We fell into a thoughtful silence, and then Alice asked, "So, why didn't Carlton tell the police he was having an affair with Paula?"

"Possibly to protect her? He thought it was all over with Paula—he was sure she would believe he was guilty. He thought Adam must have gone back and killed Harper because of Sonia and he didn't blame him for doing so—in fact, he could easily have done it

[144]

himself—in a sense he felt he <u>was</u> guilty. He may as well go to prison for a crime Adam committed.

"Blimey," said Jill. "And I thought he was just a really good cook!"

Chapter 21

The following morning Carlton was released. Adam was re-interviewed. The police decided not to pursue charges for the assault on Harper but gave them both cautions.

Okay, I admit, there were a few assumptions which I'd made when I explained things to the others. Paula and Carlton came over, so I was able to talk it through. It turned out that I'd got it almost right. After they'd beaten him up, they didn't leave him out in the woods—they took him back to Red Rum. Then Carlton went back to Bobby Dazzler. Adam was the last to leave. He was wearing gloves, so he left no prints. When I found Harper's body, Carlton assumed Adam had murdered him, as I had guessed, so when he was arrested, he clammed up.

"But it was a murder, Carlton, even if you suspected a mate, you should have told the police," I said.

He pursed his lips, and I thought he wasn't going to reply. Paula put her hand on his arm.

"When I was arrested, it was like Iraq all over again. Speaking out then did me no good—no-one listened. It was all political, and no-one cared about what really happened. I guess I'd given up."

"So it wasn't because you thought it was over with Paula."

They smiled at each other and kissed.

Then he asked, "What's that?"

"What's what?" I answered, trying to see where he was looking.

He picked up the amulet from the bookcase.

"This." He held it up to show me, then scrutinised it carefully.

"Oh, I found it in the long barrow."

He looked at me frowning. "The long barrow? Really?"

"Someone must have dropped it. A bit of tourist tat, but I like it."

He looked at me. There was a glint in his eye.

"Come on," he jumped up. "We're going up to the long barrow. I need to show you something."

I popped over to Freda to see whether I could borrow a torch. The batteries had given up on mine. She asked Carlton what we were looking for, but he refused to say anything further. Intrigued, she decided to come with us. I was glad that I'd have her with me. To be honest, I wasn't looking forward to going back there.

When we got up to the barrow, Carlton headed straight for the main chamber.

"Show me where you were."

I headed over to the far side, by the wall. Being there again sent a shiver down my spine.

"I was here."

"Do you mind telling us what happened?"

"I—erm," I hesitated. "It's all a bit mixed up." Truth be told, what had actually happened seemed even more real to me now, as I stood there than it had at the time.

"I was standing here, and after I bit Danny, he threw me against

[147]

the wall—somewhere here, I guess." I leaned down. "I must have felt it, in the dark and grabbed it."

I wasn't at all convinced by what I was saying, but it sounded plausible enough. I didn't want to say anything about the weird vision, or dream or whatever it had been. The only person I ever told that to was Charlie.

"Wow!" Carlton exclaimed. "So it was lying on the floor?"

"I, er, don't know. I guess so. Why?"

"Well, first, looking at the silver, and workmanship, I'm pretty sure it's genuine—an expert would confirm. But have a look at this." He stepped into the centre of the passage. "Do you remember, Madison, I told you that during the original excavation, two skeletons were found, hand in hand? They were lying here," he indicated along the chamber.

"Oh? I imagined them being further up towards the end."

"No, it was here. Look at this. Shine your torch across that wall, along the face of those stones, next to where you were throw down."

I angled the light as he indicated.

"Most people miss this—as you have to have the light exactly right," explained Carlton.

"Oh, wow!"

The light revealed an almost life-size drawing, etched onto the stone wall, of a male and a female, crude but clear. It was easy to miss, but with the light at the right angle, it leapt out at me. I adjusted the beam for best effect.

"Now look here."

I knelt down to look more closely where he pointed.

A thin cord was drawn hanging from the lovers' hands. On the end of it was an amulet. My heart missed a beat. I looked at Carlton, and he handed me the amulet I had found. I placed it on the one in the drawing, and it matched perfectly, in pattern and size.

I gasped, and Carlton explained, "You can see the image shows them holding an amulet. As there was never one found, the archaeologists came to the conclusion that either it never existed, or that it was stolen by grave robbers. It looks like it did exist—and you found it."

I was confused. I stood up and looked at the two faces in the drawing. Were these the ones I had seen? The drawings were so crude and worn that it wasn't possible to make out any useful detail. Whether I had seen a vision or passed out, I had no idea. I stroked each of the roughly drawn faces of the couple. Whatever had happened, I would never forget them.

Chapter 22

Three weeks later, I was explaining everything to an amazed and slightly jealous Isla.

"I can't believe that I go away for a holiday, and all this happens. So Danny's up for murder?"

"Yes, he's been charged, and his trial's been fixed for next September. He's expected to plead guilty."

"And Carlton?"

"He's moved in with Paula," I smiled, "I don't know what they'll do with Bobby Dazzler. And Adam and Jill are going to find somewhere else to moor. Too many memories here. They've already put Red Rum up for sale."

"Not surprised. Shame, though, I like Jill." She paused and tickled Ember, who was delighted to have her mistress back. "Apart from all the excitement you've been having, how did you get on with the boat?"

"Isla, I loved it. I mean, really loved it," I gushed.

"Oh, good. If you ever need to get away again, you can come and stay with me."

"Thanks. I've decided though—I'm going to buy my own boat."

"You are? You liked it that much?"

"Yeah!" I laughed. "I phoned Charlie at the marina and asked him to look out for one for me. He rang me yesterday and said there's one I need to have a look at. We're going next week. It's called Peggity Sue."

"Cool name—but you need to look at lots before you decide."

"Oh, I know. I'm going to look at hundreds. It'll be great fun."

"Helloo," called a Scottish voice.

"Hi, Freda, come in," said Isla.

"I wanted to let you know—in honour of your return, Isla, and to celebrate, Carlton is cooking a meal for us all tonight."

"Oh, fantastic!"

"Celebrate what?" Isla asked.

That evening the restaurant was closed to the public, so we had it to ourselves. Carlton and Paula cooked and served, although each of us insisted on helping where we could. We were all happily chatting and exchanging stories. I watched Jill and Adam as they smiled at each other and kissed from time to time. Even Rose looked relaxed. Veronica and Alice sat either side of her, showing off new hairstyles.

While we were all tucking into the main course, Carlton called for silence, got on one knee, and asked Paula to marry him. She said yes, as soon as the divorce came through, which made us all laugh and applaud. Carlton and Paula insisted everyone would be invited to their wedding.

It would soon be time for me to leave. I was certainly going to miss my new-found friends.

The End

If you enjoyed Murder in Mercury,

then you'll love Madison's next adventure

'Murder at the Marina'.

Keep reading this book to enjoy the opening chapters.

'Murder at the Marina'

Prologue

Melbourne Australia

Eve could not believe what she was seeing.

Twenty years of buried fears, terrors, confusion, and utter desperation came flooding back in a moment.

"Are you alright?" Lilly asked.

The voice failed to penetrate the bubble that had enveloped her.

"Madam, are you alright? You're looking pale."

Lilly's hand resting on her shoulder shook her back into her bedroom.

"Oh, yes, sorry. I'm fine. Thank you."

But she was not fine. She was not fine at all. She had not been fine from the moment she saw who had stepped out of the car, now parked on her drive. It had made her blood run cold.

"Oh, look, you've got a visitor," Lilly said brightly as she looked over her shoulder. "Shall I go and see what he wants?"

All the years that had passed. All the water that had flowed under the bridge. All the pain that had been buried, and here he was, large as life, walking up to her front door.

"Madam?"

"Oh! Yes—erm—no, I—I know him. Show him into the drawing-room, please. Tell him I'll be down shortly."

Her heart was racing. She was feeling faint, hot, nauseous. She looked towards the en-suite. After a few breaths, the queasy feeling began to pass a little. She sat on one of the leather wing chairs next to the balcony door of her bedroom. She had been so thrilled when she found a set of four beautiful chairs at the bargain price of ten thousand dollars plus shipping from Adelaide. Her late husband, her patient, lovely, long-suffering, beautiful Curtis, had smiled when she had excitedly shown him. They were the final touch to complete the re-modelling of the master bedroom. He kissed her and asked if she would like to fly over to see them before ordering. She had decided not to but contacted the seller who arranged a Skype tour of the chairs for her.

Those memories were forgotten as she thought about the man who, at this precise moment, was being shown in. That man took her back to a dark time, long before she had met her late husband.

Her hands were shaking. She placed them firmly on her lap. She took a deep breath. She could do this. Whatever he wanted, she would face him and get rid of him as quickly as she could.

"Well, hello Eve. Nice digs. You done good," he said in his familiar Australian drawl. He was looking around the room while absently dragging on a cigarette.

"Lilly," she called, "find an ashtray, please."

"Ashtray?"

"Oh, a bowl or saucer, one from the blue set will do."

[154]

He sat down on a three thousand dollar settee that she had brought back from Italy. An unbelievable find she had made during a holiday. Lilly returned and placed a highly polished occasional table next to him, added an Amara coaster from their Fornasetti range and a saucer from the blue set. Scott immediately stubbed out his cigarette and went to light another. She almost told him not to smoke in the house but thought better of it. She sat on a lounge chair at an appropriate distance.

"Didn't think you'd see me again, eh?" He took a long drag and blew the smoke up towards the chandelier. "I'll have a whisky, by the way," he added.

She didn't move.

"Scott, why are you here?"

He seemed almost surprised at the question as if the answer should have been obvious. "I saw the obituary of y' old man and came to pay my respects."

She said nothing. Respect was a word she had never associated with him.

She went over to the reproduction Georgian sideboard, poured him a whisky and herself a vodka, and sat down again.

He took a swig, stood up, and walked over to the large bi-fold doors overlooking the grounds and the bay beyond.

"It's a beautiful house, Eve, great views."

She wondered where this was heading.

"You've done well for yourself." He looked over to her, "Or, should I say that you married well? That would be more accurate."

[155]

"Excuse me a moment." She made her way to the kitchen, and said quietly so as not to be overheard, "Lilly, if he's still in there in ten minutes can you come and tell me that I need to get ready for my appointment, please?"

"Appointment? Oh, yes, of course. Is everything alright?"

"It will be when he's gone."

Back in the drawing-room, Scott was sitting again, watching her return, with dark, slightly watery eyes. The eyes were still unmistakable. The same eyes that had drawn her in all those years ago. The same eyes that repulsed her so much now. He leaned back and crossed his legs in an affectedly relaxed manner.

"So, do y' hear much from your first husband?"

"Really? Seriously?"

"Well I don't know, do I? As soon as I was locked up, he took you and buggered off. Never a visit, never so much as a letter."

She tried not to show a reaction as a sharp pain stabbed her heart at the forgotten memory. She could feel tears rising. She would not cry.

"Well, don't look at me like that," he said, stubbing out his cigarette. "You abandoned me, and as I heard it, you went and abandoned him."

"I'm not coming back to you if that's what you're asking." She wasn't at all clear what he was trying to say. Even back in the day, he had favoured strange melodramatic asides as a way of intimidating people, but often they only found him confusing.

"God, no! That's not it," he laughed. "We're way beyond that."

"It's been lovely catching up, but I have things to do." She moved to get up, but he reached out a hand and indicated for her to stay.

"Felix and I have, erm, business to sort out, and I'm going to sort it. You left him for whatever reason. You want in?" He looked at his glass. "That's all, an offer, for old time's sake."

He pulled out another cigarette from the pack and tapped it idly on the occasional table.

"I've no problem with Felix. Can you not smoke in here!"

She wanted him out.

He lit up anyway, then reached into his pocket, took something out and threw it on the floor at her feet.

She recognised it immediately.

"Oh my God!" she said. She leaned forward and picked up the small jewellery box. "It's the necklace and earring set Felix gave me." She took out the necklace and stared at it, turning it over and over. The diamonds glinted and winked at her. Old friends. "The last time I saw these was in England. How did you get them?"

"Ways and means. Thought you might want 'em back," he smirked.

"I don't want to get involved, Scott." She held the box up for him to take back. "Let it go. You're free now. Get on with your life."

Lilly popped her head around the door, "Excuse me, madam, but you've an appointment."

[157]

"Oh yes, thank you. I'll be up to get ready directly."

He ignored the box as he stood. "Sorry, you feel like that. Have a nice life."

She didn't move as Lilly showed him out.

"Are you alright, madam?"

Eve stared blankly into space. Occasional tears escaped and ran down her cheeks. This was completely unexpected. It was all too much.

"Get me a vodka, Lilly." She was bearly able to control the emotion in her voice.

"Madam, please, let me make you a coffee," coaxed Lilly, handing her a tissue.

She took a deep breath. All the things that she had coped with over the years, and now this, right on top of losing Curtis, but she was no longer the depressed and confused woman of her youth. She could do this.

"Coffee it is," she said, sounding calm. Then suddenly, her expression altered.

"Oh!" she exclaimed. Her hand flew to her mouth, and she stared wide-eyed at Lilly.

"What, madam?"

"If he goes after Felix, what about my daughter?"

It took a few moments for the words to sink in.

"Madam! You have a daughter?"

Chapter 1

Tinderford, England. Two months later

Tony frowned at the sky. It was grey, overcast, and starting to drizzle, even though the forecast had been sunny. "Well, I guess it's sunny somewhere up there, past those clouds," he said to himself, silently cursing the weather app.

One of the reasons they had hired the narrowboat, at the last minute, was because the weather was supposed to be good. It would be great to get some fresh air and outdoor exercise and would get the kids away from their i-stuff for a while, but now he could barely get them out of the cabin.

"Paul, want to steer?" He called down into the boat.

No reply.

When they had started, they had been so keen to help, but the novelty soon wore off, and now they only dragged themselves away from their i-things under duress.

He pulled the hood over his head as best he could as the rain got a little harder. Rubbish mac this, he thought, too thin and clingy. There was a lock coming up. Although he could get the boat through on his own, it was always such a faff by himself. Manoeuvring and tying up, opening and closing the paddles, dealing with the heavy gates, and clambering up and down the wet, slippery lock ladders. The last straw was having to moor up again after he'd left the lock, to go back and close the gates behind him. It could actually be quite pleasant if he were able to stay on the boat while the kids did the paddles and gates for him.

He leaned down to the door of the cabin again. "Lock ahead!" He called. No response. This must be a good reception area if they were both still playing games.

"Hey, guys!" He shouted again.

"Eh?" Came a reply.

"Lock ahead!"

Lucy appeared, "Is it lunchtime yet? I'm hungry."

"There's a lock ahead. Tell Paul, and I'll drop you both at the landing."

"Oh, not another one. Paul, you're needed!" she called as she headed back into the boat.

"Don't you go anywhere. You can help too."

"This is a pain, Dad!"

He dropped them at the lock landing and watched as they sulkily wandered up to the lock gates. They were moaning incessantly about getting wet, yet neither had bothered with a coat. Typical. Tony kept an eye on what they were doing. He didn't want a repeat of that first disastrous lock, but he could see that they had checked this time, and the paddles at the other end were closed.

As he waited for them to do their worst, he looked around. The lock was in the middle of nowhere, with no buildings or roads for miles. It was a beautiful part of the canal, even in the rain. So peaceful, no people, only wildlife. There had been a fantastic heron earlier, standing on the bank perfectly still, on its over-long legs. He also watched for kingfishers, as he had read that they could sometimes be seen on this part of the canal. The wildlife had been a highlight of the holiday so far. What a shame the kids weren't getting it.

The gates opened, and he took the boat in. The kids closed the gates and, to their credit, operated the paddles gently, so the water didn't churn too wildly as the lock filled. Soon everyone was back on board, and they were on their way again.

A short while later they passed a boat tied up all by itself in a perfect mooring spot. Tony slowed right down to tick-over as usual. He used to think, naively, that going too fast made boats rock, so things fell off shelves, but now he knew that this only happened if you actually bumped into one. During the last week, he had found out that if you go too fast, your wake could be powerful enough to pull another boat right off its mooring. He'd already seen seasoned boaters re-fixing a narrowboat whose mooring pins had been dragged out of the bank by a speeding hire boat.

Once clear of the moored boat, he throttled the engine up again, but suddenly there was an ominous clanking and banging below his feet. Tony quickly knocked the throttle back to neutral. The noise was loud enough to startle the kids. Despite their distractions, they both appeared at the door, moving more quickly than they had all day.

"What was that?" Lucy asked.

"Are we sinking?" Paul asked.

"No, we're not," replied Tony, "I don't know what it was, but I didn't like the sound of it. I'll try again."

"No, hang on, dad," said Paul, "try it in reverse. If the prop's tangled with weeds, it might free it."

[161]

He moved the control the other way, but it was clear from the clunking and juddering that something was still wrong.

Paul knelt and leaned over the back. "Yeah, I reckon the prop's all jammed up. There's a load of stuff down there," he said, getting back up.

"Oh damn, we're drifting," said Tony, looking around. "What do we do now?"

Sure enough, the boat was slowly turning at an angle across the canal.

"Call that number they gave us at the marina," said Lucy.

Tony got his phone out, "No signal! What about you guys?"

"We've got no signal, either."

"I thought you were playing games?"

"We were but with each other over Bluetooth," said Paul.

"We've had no signal for hours," added Lucy with a sigh, "it's so lame!"

Suddenly a small voice piped up, "You stuck?"

They all looked over to the towpath where a girl about five years old, in wellies and a mac, was standing watching them, waving a stick around absent-mindedly.

"It's alright thanks, we'll sort it," said Paul.

"Thing is, though," said Lucy to no-one in particular, "how?"

Tony took off his jacket and rolled up his sleeves, "Paul, get that long pole that's up on the roof, and use it to keep us off the opposite bank and as straight as you can, okay? Lucy, you stand here and move the tiller out of the way when I ask you."

Tony lay on the deck and stretched over the back so he could reach down below the water to the propeller. He could just about feel trapped debris. "If I can clear some of this we might be able to get going again." He spent a couple of minutes trying to angle himself, so he could reach around and under the end of the boat, while Lucy kept the rudder clear from where he was trying to work.

"Hey, mister," came the small voice from the bank.

He ignored it and carried on. He needed to lean over a little more.

"Mister!"

He wrapped one arm around the base of the tiller. This enabled him to lean further, with his face almost at the waterline. He could feel the propeller and some of the stuff around it, but he couldn't get enough purchase to free anything.

"Scoose me, mister," came the annoying voice, "You're doing it wrong! You'll hurt yourself."

Tony pulled himself back and gave his cold, soaking arm a shake. He had to admit she was right. His ribs were already aching. "Suppose you're an expert, are you?" He spoke tersely, and a little more rudely than he intended.

"You're lying on it!" She shouted as she bashed her stick on the ground in frustration.

"What?"

"Lift up the floor you're standing on. Open the wee-catch. It's a box thing!"

[163]

"The wee-catch?"

"Didn't someone mention that at the marina?" chipped in Lucy.

"Yeah, they might have, they said so much I've forgotten most of it."

He realised he would never clear the propeller leaning over the back anyway. He stood up and lifted the end section of the deck board. Lo and behold, underneath there was a large grey metal box.

"Turn the big turny thing," she ordered.

Tony scratched his head. There was a large clamp that was clearly meant to be undone. He looked at the girl, then at the 'turny thing'. "Oh well," he mumbled, "here goes nothing." He reached down and with a bit of effort managed to twist the handle, which loosened the clamp around a box.

"Slide it off and open the lid," shouted the girl.

He did as she said and heaved off the cover. Below was a perfect rectangle of dark canal water.

"Got it," he shouted back.

"Now get the yucky stuff off the prop!"

He could see nothing but murky water, but as he stuck his hand in and felt around, he soon touched the propeller blade. It was much easier to reach now. He found his bearings and was able to make a little sense of the junk that was tangled around it. With some effort and quite a lot of swearing to himself, he managed to clear it all, making a small pile of wet rubbish on the deck. The bulk of it turned out to be the stringy remains of a farmer's seed sack, but there were some slimy clumps of reed too.

"You okay, mate?" asked another voice.

Tony looked up, and an older boy, a teenager, had joined the girl on the towpath.

The girl turned to the boy, "He's doing the wee-catch. Don't think he's done it before."

"Weed hatch," corrected the boy.

"That's what I said," replied the girl.

"You done it?" the boy asked.

"Yup, it all seems clear now," said Tony.

"When you put the lid back on, make sure it's good 'n straight. And make that clamp tight. Boats sink if it's not on right," the boy said.

Tony followed the instructions, and it all seemed to go back correctly.

Paul had done a great job fending the boat off the bank. When Tony fired up the engine and pushed the control into drive, to his great relief, the boat crept forward with no distressing noises.

"Pull over here," said the boy, "I'll check it if you like."

Tony did like, as clearly he, and even his little sister, knew far more about all of this than he did. He guided the boat over to the bank. All four kids enthusiastically moored up, the two young professionals showing the two novices how to hammer the mooring pins in more securely, and the best way to tie the ropes. Tony stood by the tiller grinning to himself.

"Sorry if they've been annoying you." A female voice came suddenly from behind, making him jump.

He turned to find a young woman walking up the towpath, and a small dog racing ahead towards the children.

She was in her mid-twenties, her short auburn hair was topped by a smart blue trilby hat, not ideal against the rain, but her sensible rain mac made up for it. Overall she was much better dressed for the weather than he was and certainly seemed to mind it less. He noticed that she walked with a slight limp.

"Oh, no. They saved us," Tony grinned.

"We're back there in Peggity Sue," she said, waving towards the moored boat they had passed earlier. She smiled a broad contagious smile which Tony instantly found engaging and warm.

"I'm Madison," she said. "Madison Leigh."

To continue enjoying this book read

'Murder at the Marina'